Vito was asking Holly to marry him… He was actually asking her to marry him! How was she supposed to react to that when she had been astonished by his proposal?

'You should also consider the reality that eventually our son will be very rich, and growing up outside *my* world isn't the best preparation for that day,' Vito pointed out. 'I want to be his father. A father who is there for Angelo when he needs me. A benefit neither you nor I enjoyed.'

He was making very valid points, but Holly felt harassed and intimidated rather than grateful for his honesty. 'But *marriage*?' she reasoned. 'That's such a huge decision.'

'And a decision only you can make. But there would be other benefits for you,' Vito told her quietly. 'You could set up as an interior designer and live your dream with me—'

'You're starting to sound like a trained negotiator,' Holly cut in.

'I *am* a trained negotiator,' Vito conceded. 'But I want to give our son the very best start in life he can have—with a genuine family.'

And that was the real moment when Holly veered from consternation and fell deep into his honey trap.

Christmas with a Tycoon

Mediterranean billionaires under the mistletoe

Christmas might be a time for giving, but these billionaires are thinking only of what they can take!

Vito Zaffari might have a ruthless reputation, but when Holly crashes his festive hideaway she leaves with an unexpected Christmas gift…

Apollo Metraxis has made a career of bachelorhood, but the conditions of his father's will force him to choose a bride. Pixie might be the last wife he'd ever choose, but she's soon the only one he wants!

Don't miss either of these fabulous festive stories!

The Italian's Christmas Child
November 2016

The Greek's Christmas Bride
December 2016

THE ITALIAN'S CHRISTMAS CHILD

BY
LYNNE GRAHAM

MILLS & BOON

First Published in Great Britain 2016
By Mills & Boon, an imprint of HarperCollins*Publishers*
1 London Bridge Street, London, SE1 9GF

© 2016 Lynne Graham

ISBN: 978-0-263-06561-9

Our policy is to use papers that are natural, renewable and recyclable products and made from wood grown in sustainable forests. The logging and manufacturing processes conform to the legal environmental regulations of the country of origin.

Printed and bound in Great Britain
by CPI Antony Rowe, Chippenham, Wiltshire

Lynne Graham was born in Northern Ireland and has been a keen romance reader since her teens. She is very happily married to an understanding husband who has learned to cook since she started to write! Her five children keep her on her toes. She has a very large dog who knocks everything over, a very small terrier who barks a lot, and two cats. When time allows, Lynne is a keen gardener.

Visit the Author Profile page at millsandboon.co.uk for more titles.

Christmas is one of my favourite times of year.
It's about family and friends, so this is dedicated to you.

CHAPTER ONE

THE MOORLAND LANDSCAPE on Dartmoor was cold and crisp with ice. As the four-wheel drive turned off the road onto a rough lane, Vito saw the picturesque cottage sheltering behind winter-bare trees with graceful frosted branches. His lean, strong face grim with exhaustion, he got out of the car ahead of his driver, only tensing as he heard the sound of yet another text hitting his phone. Ignoring it, he walked into the property while the driver emptied the car.

Instant warmth greeted him and he raked a weary hand through the dense blue-black hair that the breeze had whipped across his brow. There was a welcome blaze in the brick inglenook fireplace and he fought the sense of relief threatening to engulf him. He was not a coward. He had not run away as his ex-fiancée had accused him of doing. He would have stood his ground and stayed in Florence had he not finally appreciated that the pursuit of the paparazzi and outrageous headlines were only being fuelled by his continuing presence.

He had grudgingly followed his best friend Apollo's advice and had removed himself from the scene, recognising that his mother had quite enough to deal with when her husband was in hospital following a serious heart attack without also having to suffer the embarrassment of her son's newly acquired notoriety. Undeniably, his friend had much more experience than Vito had of handling scandals and bad publicity. The Greek playboy had led a far less restricted life than Vito, who had known from an early age that he would become the next CEO of the Zaffari Bank. His grandfather had steeped him in the history and traditions of a family that could trace its beginnings back to the Middle Ages when the Zaffari name had stood shoulder to shoulder with words like *honour* and *principle*. No more, Vito reflected wryly. Now he would be famous for ever as the banker who had indulged in drugs and strippers.

Not his style, not his style at all, Vito ruminated ruefully, breaking free of his thoughts to lavishly tip his driver and thank him. When it came to the drug allegations, he could only suppress a groan. One of his closest friends at school had taken something that had killed him at a party and Vito had never been tempted by illegal substances. And the whores? In truth Vito could barely remember when he had last had sex. Although he had been engaged until a week earlier, Marzia had always been cool in that department.

'She's a lady to her backbone.' His grandfather had sighed approvingly, shortly before his passing. 'A Ravello with the right background and breeding. She will make a superb hostess and future mother for your children.'

Not now, though, Vito thought, glancing at his phone to discover that his ex had sent him yet another text. *Dio mio*, what did she want from him now? He had perfectly understood her decision to break off their engagement and he had wasted no time in putting the house she had been furnishing for their future occupation back on the market. That, however, had proved to be a move that had evidently rankled, even though he had assured Marzia that she was welcome to keep every stick of furniture in the place.

What about the Abriano painting? she'd texted.

He pointed out that his grandfather's engagement gift would have to be returned. It was worth millions—how much more compensation was he to pay in terms of damages? He had offered her the house but she had refused it.

But in spite of his generosity, he still felt guilty. He had messed up Marzia's life and embarrassed her. For probably the first time in his life he had wronged someone. On the spur of the moment he had made a decision that had hit Marzia very hard and even the sincerest apology could not lessen the impact of it. But he could not have told his former fiancée the truth because he could not have trusted her to keep it secret. And if the truth came out, his sacrifice would be pointless and it would plunge the only woman he had ever loved into gross humiliation and heartbreak. Vito had made a very tough choice and he was fully prepared to take the heat for it.

That, indeed, was why vanishing off-grid for a couple of weeks over Christmas *still* felt disturbingly gutless to Vito, whose natural instincts were pre-emptive and forceful.

'Ritchie's a lying, cheating scumbag!' Holly's flatmate and best friend, Pixie, ranted furiously down the phone.

Holly grimaced and pushed her hand through her

heavy mane of black curling hair, her big blue eyes red-rimmed and sad as she checked her watch to see that she was still safely within her lunch hour. 'You're not going to get any argument from me on that score,' she said ruefully.

'He's as bad as that last guy who borrowed all the money from you,' Pixie reminded her with a typical lack of tact. 'And the one before that who wanted to marry you so that you could act as a carer for his invalid mother!'

Wincing at her disheartening past history with men, Holly reflected that she could not have done worse in the dating stakes had she drawn up a specific list of selfish, dishonest losers. 'Let's not look back,' she urged, keen to move on to more positive subjects.

Pixie refused to cooperate, saying, 'So, what on earth are you planning to do now for your festive break with me, stuck in London and Ritchie out of the picture?'

A sudden grin lit Holly's oval face with surprising enthusiasm. 'I'm going to make Christmas for Sylvia instead!'

'But she's staying with her daughter in Yorkshire over the holiday...*isn't she*?'

'No, Alice had to cancel Sylvia at the last minute. Her house has been flooded by a burst pipe. Sylvia was horribly disappointed when she found out and then when I walked in on Ritchie with his floozy today, I realised that I could take two pieces of bad luck and make something good out of them...'

'I really hate it when you pick yourself up off the floor and come over all optimistic again.' Pixie sighed dramatically. 'Please tell me you at least *thumped* Ritchie...'

'I told him what I thought of him…briefly,' Holly qualified with her innate honesty, for really she had been too squeamish to linger in the presence of her half-naked boyfriend and the woman he had chosen to cheat on her with. 'So, is it all right for me to borrow your car to go to Sylvia's?'

'Of course it is. How else would you get there? But watch out: there's snow forecast—'

'They always like to talk about snow this close to Christmas,' Holly demurred, unimpressed by the threat. 'By the way, I'm taking our Christmas tree and ornaments with me and I'd already bought and made all the trimmings for a festive lunch. I'm going to put on that Santa outfit you wore for the Christmas party at the salon last year. Sylvia loves a laugh. She'll appreciate it.'

'Sylvia will be over the moon when she finds you on the doorstep,' her friend predicted warmly. 'Between losing her husband and having to move because she couldn't manage the farmhouse alone any more, she's had a horrible year.'

Holly held firmly on to the inspiring prospect of her foster mother's happiness at her arrival while she finished her afternoon shift at the busy café where she worked. It was Christmas Eve and she adored the festive season, possibly because she had grown up mainly in foster care and had always been painfully conscious that she did not have a real family to share the experience with. In an effort to comfort her, Pixie had assured her that family Christmases could be a nightmare and that she was in love with an ideal of Christmas rather than the reality. But some day, somehow, Holly was determined to turn fantasy into reality with a husband and children of her own. That was her dream and in spite of recent setbacks she understood that it was hanging on to her dream that essentially kept her going through more challenging times.

Both she and Pixie had been fostered by Sylvia Ware from the age of twelve and the older woman's warm acceptance and understanding had been far superior to the uncaring and occasionally neglectful homes Holly and Pixie had endured as younger children caught up in the care system. Holly had long regretted not paying more heed to Sylvia's lectures about studying harder at school. Over the years Holly had attended so many different schools and made so many moves that she had simply drifted through her education, accepting that she would always be behind in certain subjects. Now at almost twenty-four, Holly had redressed that adolescent mistake by attending night classes to achieve basic qualifications but the road ahead to further education seemed so long and complex that it daunted her and she had instead chosen to study for a qualification in interior design online.

'And what use is that to you?' Pixie, who was a hairdresser, had asked baldly.

'I'm really interested in it. I love looking at a room and thinking about how I can improve it.'

'But people from our sort of background don't get hired as interior designers,' Pixie had pointed out. 'I mean, we're just ordinary workers trying to pay our bills, not people with fancy careers.'

And Holly had to acknowledge as she donned her friend's Santa outfit that there *was* nothing fancy or impressive about her likely to combat that discouraging assurance. Fortunately the short dress had been far too generously sized on her infinitely more slender friend.

Pixie might envy Holly's curves but Pixie could eat whatever she liked and never put on a pound while Holly was engaged in a constant struggle to prevent her curves from taking over. Her golden skin tone hailed from an unknown father. He might or might not have been someone her erratic mother had met abroad. On the other hand he might simply have been a man who lived in the same street. Her only parent had told her so many lies that Holly had long accepted that the truth of her fatherhood would never be known.

At four feet ten inches tall, Holly, like her mother, lacked height. She pulled on warm black winter tights under the bright red satin and corseted dress. Thrusting her feet into cowboy boots rather than the heels Pixie had sported for her party a year earlier, Holly scowled at her gaudy, busty reflection in the mirror and jammed on the Santa hat in a defiant move. OK, she looked comical, she acknowledged, but her appearance would make Sylvia laugh and overlook the disappointment of not having her own daughters around her to celebrate Christmas Day with, and that was what was truly important.

Planning to spend the night on the sofa in Sylvia's tiny living area, she packed her rucksack and carefully placed what remained of the decorations and the food into a box heavy enough to make her stagger on her final trip to the car. *At least the food wouldn't be going to waste*, she thought with determined positivity, until a flashback of the ugly scene she had interrupted with Ritchie and the receptionist at his insurance office cut through her rebellious brain.

Her tummy rolled with nausea and her battered heart clenched. *In the middle of the day as well*, she thought with a shudder. She couldn't imagine even having sex, never mind going at it on a desk in broad daylight. Possibly she wasn't a very adventurous person. In fact both she and Pixie were probably pretty strait-laced. At twelve years old they had shuddered over the ugly chaos of broken relationships in their mothers' lives and had solemnly decided to swear off men altogether. Of course once puberty had kicked in, with all its attendant confusing hormones, that rule had failed. At fourteen they had ditched their embargo on men while deciding that sex was the real danger and best avoided outside a serious relationship. *A serious committed relationship.* Holly's eyes rolled at the memory of their mutual innocence. And so far neither she nor her friend had managed to have a serious committed relationship with a man.

All that considered thought about steering clear of sexual relationships hadn't done her many favours either, Holly reflected with helpless insecurity. There had been men she really liked who ran a mile from what they saw as her outdated expectations and then there had been the others who stayed around for a few weeks or months, eager to be the first into her bed. Had she only ever been a sexual challenge to Ritchie? How long, for instance, had he been messing around with other women?

'Did you expect me to wait for you for ever?' Ritchie had shouted back at her, blaming her for his betrayal because she had held back on having sex with him. 'What's so special about you?'

Holly flinched at that ugly recollection because she had always known that there was nothing particularly special about her.

It was snowing as she drove off in the battered little hatchback that Pixie had christened Clementine, and she groaned. She loved the look of snow but she didn't like to drive in it and she hated being cold. Thank goodness for the car, she acknowledged, as she rattled out of the small Devon town where she lived and worked.

Snow was falling fast by the time she reached Sylvia's home, which was dismayingly dark. Perhaps the older woman was out at a church service or visiting a neighbour. Jamming down her hat over the mass of hair fighting to escape its confines, Holly rapped on the door and waited, stamping her feet to keep warm. After a couple of minutes she knocked again and then she followed the communal path to the little house next door, which was brightly lit, and knocked there instead.

'I'm sorry to bother you but I wondered if you knew where Mrs Ware has gone and if she'll be home soon,' Holly asked with a friendly smile.

'Sylvia left this afternoon. I helped her pack—she was in such a tizzy because she wasn't expecting anyone,' the elderly little woman at the door told her.

Holly frowned, her heart sinking. 'So, she went to her daughter's after all, then?'

'Oh, no, it wasn't the daughter who came, it was her son. Big tall chap in a suit. He's taking her back to Bruges or Belgium or some place,' the neighbour told her less certainly.

'Brussels. That's where Stephen lives. Do you know how long she'll be away?'

'A couple of weeks at least, she seemed to think…'

As deflated as a pricked balloon, Holly walked back to her car.

'You watch yourself driving home,' the old lady called after her. 'There's to be heavy snow tonight.'

'Thanks, I will,' Holly promised, forcing a smile. 'Merry Christmas!'

And a very merry Christmas it was going to be on her own, she thought unhappily, annoyed to find that her eyes were prickling with tears. After all, Sylvia was going to have the best possible Christmas with her son and the grandchildren she rarely saw. Holly was really, really pleased that Stephen had swooped in from abroad to save the day. He and his wife were rare visitors but he had at least made the effort and now his mother wouldn't have to spend her first Christmas as a widow alone. Holly sniffed and blinked back the tears, scolding herself for being so selfish. She was young and healthy and employed. She had nothing to complain about, nothing at all.

Maybe she was simply missing Pixie, she reasoned, as she drove with care on the steep, icy road that climbed up over the moors. Pixie's kid brother was in some sort of trouble and Pixie had taken time off to go and stay with him and sort it out. It was probably financial trouble but Holly wouldn't ask any awkward questions or offer unwelcome advice because she didn't want to hurt her friend, who was deeply attached to her horribly self-centred sibling. Everyone had problems, she reminded herself doggedly, tensing as she felt the tyres of the car shift into a near skid on the slippery surface and slowing her speed even more. She had far fewer problems than most people and had no excuse whatsoever for feeling sorry for herself.

Ritchie? Well, that wasn't an excuse. So, she had got hurt but then Pixie would point out that she was too soft in that line, too prone to thinking well of people and being knocked back hard when they let her down. Pixie was more of a cynic, strong on distrust as a means of self-defence, except when it came to her own brother.

Holly peered out of the windscreen because visibility was fading fast with the wipers unable to keep up with the heavy snow. She wasn't the dramatic type, she assured herself, as the car coasted down a hill that seemed steeper than it had seemed when she drove over it earlier that evening, but the weather was foul and the light snowfall she had dimly expected now bore a closer resemblance to a blizzard.

And then without the smallest warning, and to the accompaniment of her strangled scream, the car glided in the most terrifying slow motion off the road into a ditch where it tilted over and wedged fast with a loud, nerve-racking crunch of metal. After switching off the engine, Holly breathed in slow and deep to calm herself. She was alive, no other car was involved and nobody was hurt. There was much to be thankful for, she told herself bracingly.

Sadly that was a conviction that took a beating once she climbed out with some difficulty, owing to the angle the car had crashed at, to inspect the damage. The side wing of Pixie's elderly vehicle was crushed up against a large rock, which had presumably been placed to mark the entrance to the lane. *My goodness, how much will the repairs cost?* was her first fearful thought. It was *her* responsibility, not Pixie's.

A spark of fear assailed her only after she had examined her surroundings. The road was deserted and lay under a covering of unbroken snow. It was a bad night and it was Christmas Eve and she didn't think there would be much passing traffic, if any. As she stood there nursing her mobile phone and wondering what she was going to do, Holly had never felt more lonely. She had no close friend she could ring and drag out in such dreadful weather on such a special night. No, she was on her own, sink or swim. Consternation gripped her when she couldn't get a signal on her phone to use it. Only then did she turn round to look again at the lane she stood beside and there, like a faint beacon in the darkness, she saw the lights of what could only be a house and relief filled her to overflowing. Hopefully it was occupied and the occupant had a landline she could use to call for a breakdown truck.

Vito was savouring a glass of award-winning wine and wondering what to do with the evening when the knocker on the door sounded. Taken aback, he frowned because he hadn't heard a car and there were no lights outside. Did the local caretaker live within walking distance? He peered out through the spyhole and saw a red-and-white Santa hat. Someone was definitely at the wrong house because Vito hated Christmas. He yanked open the door and enormous blue eyes like velvet pansies looked up at him. At first he thought his visitor was a child and then his eyes dropped and took in the swell of breasts visible between the parted edges of her coat and he registered that, although she might be very small, she was all woman.

Holly stared up in wonderment at the male who appeared in the doorway. He looked like every fantasy male she had ever dreamt about meeting all rolled into one spectacular package. In fact he was so gorgeous with his black hair, designer stubble and dark, deep-set, mysterious eyes that he made her teeth clench in dismay because he didn't look approachable or helpful or anything that might have encouraged her. That he wore a very formal dark business suit with a white shirt and natty gold tie didn't help to relax her either.

'If you're looking for a party, you're at the wrong house,' Vito told her loftily, recalling his friend's warnings about how sneaky the paparazzi could be. If he'd thought about that risk, he wouldn't have answered the door at all.

'I'm looking for a phone. Mine has no reception here and my car went off the road at the foot of your lane,' Holly explained in a rush. 'Do you have a landline?'

Exasperation flashed through Vito, who had far too much sensitive information on his cell phone to consider loaning it to anyone. 'This isn't my house. I'll look and see,' he fielded drily.

As he turned on his heel without inviting her in out of the heavily falling snow, Holly grimaced and shivered because she wasn't dressed for bad weather, having only thrown on a raincoat to cover her outfit because she had known she would be warm inside the car. *Not Mr Nice Guy, anyway*, she thought ruefully. She had recognised the impatience in those electrifyingly dark magnetic eyes, watched the flare of his nostrils and the tightening of his wide, sculpted mouth as he'd bit back a withering comment. She was good at reading faces, even gorgeous ones, she conceded, as she shifted her feet in a vain effort to heat the blood freezing in her veins. She didn't think she had ever seen a more handsome man, no, not even on a movie screen, but personality-wise she reckoned that there was a good chance that he was chillier than an icicle.

'There is a phone… You may step inside to use it,' he invited grudgingly, his foreign accent edging every syllable in a very attractive way.

Holly reddened with discomfiture, already well aware that she was not a welcome visitor. She dug out her phone to scroll through numbers for Pixie's car mechanic, Bill, who ran a breakdown service. As she did so, she missed seeing the step in front of her and tripped over it, falling forward with a force that would have knocked the breath from her body had not strong arms snapped out to catch her before she fell.

'Watch out…' Taken aback by a level of clumsiness utterly unknown to a male as surefooted as a cat, Vito virtually lifted her into the porch. As her hair briefly brushed his face he was engulfed by the scent of oranges, sweet and sun-warmed. But it was only by touching her and seeing her face below the lights that he registered that she was almost blue with cold. '*Maledizione*, you're freezing! Why didn't you tell me that?'

'It's enough of an imposition coming to the door—'

'Yes, I would surely have been happier to trip over your frozen corpse on my doorstep in the morning!' Vito fielded scathingly. 'You should've told me—'

'You've got eyes of your own and an off-putting manner. I don't like bothering people,' Holly said truthfully while she frantically rubbed her hands over her raincoat in an effort to get some feeling back into her fingers before she tried to work her phone again.

Vito gazed down at her from his height of six foot one. He was bemused by her criticism when he was trying to be pleasant and when he could not recall when a woman had last offered him a word of criticism. Even in the act of breaking their engagement, Marzia had contrived not to speak a word of condemnation. Either a woman of saintly tolerance or one who didn't give a damn who he might have slept with behind her back? It was a sobering thought.

An off-putting manner? Could that be true about him? His grandfather had taught him to maintain distance between himself and others and he had often thought that a useful gift when it came to commanding a large staff, none of whom dared to take liberties with their authoritarian CEO.

Thoroughly irritated by the thoughts awakened by his visitor and that unfamiliar self-questioning mode, he swiped the phone from between her shaking fingers and said firmly, 'Go and warm up first by the fire and then make the call.'

'Are you sure you don't mind?'

'I will contrive to bear it.'

Halfway towards the wonderful blaze of the log fire illuminating the dim interior, Holly spun round with a merriment in her eyes that lit up her whole face and she laughed. 'You're a sarky one, aren't you?'

In the firelight her eyes were bright as sapphires and that illuminating smile made the breath catch in his throat because it lent her incredible appeal. And Vito was not the sort of male who noticed women very often and when he did he usually swiftly stifled the impulse. But for a split second that playful tone and that radiant smile knocked him sideways and he found himself staring. He scanned the glorious dark hair that fell free of the Santa hat as she whipped it off, before lowering his appreciative gaze to the wonderfully generous thrust of her breasts above a neat little waist, right down to the hem of the shimmering dress that revealed slim knees and shapely calves incongruously encased in cowboy boots. He threw his shoulders back, bracing as the pulse at his groin beat out a different kind of tension.

Holly connected momentarily with eyes of gold semi-veiled by the lush black sweep of his lashes and something visceral tightened low in her pelvis as she let her attention linger on his lean, hard bone structure, which was stunningly hard and male from his level dark brows to his arrogant classic nose and his strong, sculpted jawline. Just looking at him sent the oddest flash of excitement through her and she reddened uneasily, and deliberately spun back to the fire to hold her hands out to the heat. So, he was very good-looking. That didn't mean she had to gape like an awestruck fan at a rock star, did it? She was only inside his house to use the phone, she reminded herself in embarrassment.

She flexed her fingers. 'Where did you put my phone?'

As she half turned it was settled neatly into her hand and she opened it and scrolled through the numbers. He handed her the handset of the house phone and she pressed out Bill's number, lifting it to her ear while carefully not glancing again in her host's direction.

Vito was engaged in subduing his sexual arousal and reeling in shock from the need to do so. What was he? A teenager again? She wasn't his type…if he had a type. The women in his life had invariably been tall, elegant blondes and she was very small, very curvy and very, *very* sexy, he conceded involuntarily as she moved about the room while she talked, her luxuriant hair rippling across her shoulders, her rounded hips swaying. She was apologising for disturbing someone on Christmas Eve and she apologised at great length instead of getting straight to the point of her problem with her car.

What were the chances that she was a particularly clever member of the paparazzi brigade? Vito had flown into the UK on a private plane to a private airfield and travelled to the cottage in a private car. Only Apollo and his mother, Concetta, knew where he was. But Apollo had warned him that the paps went to extraordinary lengths to steal photos and find stories they could sell. His perfect white teeth gritted. At the very least, he needed to check that there was a broken-down car at the foot of the lane.

'Boxing Day?' Holly was practically whispering in horror.

'And possibly only if the snowplough has been through ahead of me,' Bill told her apologetically. 'I'm working flat out tonight as it is. Where exactly is the car?'

The older man was local and, knowing the road well, was able to establish where she was. 'Aye, I know the house down there—foreign-owned holiday home as far as I know. And you're able to stay there?'

'Yes,' Holly said in as reassuring a tone as she could contrive while wondering if she was going to have to bed down in Pixie's car. 'Do you know anyone else I could ring?'

She tried the second number but there was no response at all. Swallowing hard, she set the digital phone down. 'I'll go back to the car now,' she told Vito squarely.

'I'll walk down with you… See if there's anything I can do—'

'Unless you have a tractor to haul it out of the ditch I shouldn't think so.' Holly buttoned her coat, tied the belt and braced herself to face the great outdoors again.

As she straightened her shoulders she looked round the room with belated admiration, suddenly noticing that the opulent décor was an amazing and highly effective marriage of traditional and contemporary styles. In spite of the ancient brick inglenook fireplace, the staircase had a glass surround and concealed lights. But she also noticed that there was one glaring omission: there were no festive decorations of any kind.

Vito yanked on his cashmere coat and scarf over the suit he still wore.

'If you don't have boots, I can't let you go down there with me… You'll get your shoes soaked,' Holly told him ruefully, glancing at the polished, city-type footwear he sported with his incredibly stylish suit, which moulded to his well-built, long-legged frame as though specifically tailored to do so.

Vito walked into the porch, which boasted a rack of boots, and, picking out a pair, donned them. Her pragmatism had secretly impressed him. Vito was extremely clever but, like many very clever people, he was not particularly practical and the challenges of rural living in bad weather lay far outside his comfort zone.

'My name is Holly,' she announced brightly on the porch.

'Vito…er… Vito Sorrentino,' Vito lied, employing his father's original surname.

His mother had been an only child, a daughter when his grandfather had longed for a son. At his grandfather's request, Vito's father had changed his name to Zaffari when he married Vito's mother to ensure that the family name would not die out. Ciccio Sorrentino had been content to surrender his name in return for the privilege of marrying a fabulously wealthy banking heiress. There was no good reason for Vito to take the risk of identifying himself to a stranger. Right now the name Zaffari was cannon fodder for the tabloids across Europe and the news of his disappearance and current location would be worth a great deal of money to a profiteer. And if there was one gift Vito had in spades it was the gilded art of making a profit and ensuring that nobody got to do it at his expense.

His grandfather would have turned in his grave at the mere threat of his grandson plunging the family name and the family bank into such a sleazy scandal. Vito, however, was rather less naive. Having attended a board meeting before his departure, Vito was aware that he could virtually do no wrong. All the Zaffari directors cared about was that their CEO continued to ensure that the Zaffari bank carried on being the most successful financial institution in Europe.

CHAPTER TWO

'YOU SAID THIS wasn't your house,' Holly reminded him through chattering teeth as they walked out into the teeth of a gale laced with snow.

'A friend loaned it to me for a break.'

'And you're staying here alone?'

'*Sì*...yes.'

'By choice...*alone*...at Christmas?' Holly framed incredulously.

'Why not?' Vito loathed Christmas but that was none of her business and he saw no need to reveal anything of a personal nature. His memories of Christmas were toxic. His parents, who rarely spent time together, had squabbled almost continuously through the festive break. His mother had made a real effort to hide that reality and make the season enjoyable, but Vito had always been far too intelligent even as a child not to understand what was happening around him. He had seen that his mother loved his father but that her love was not returned. He had watched her humiliate herself in an effort to smooth over Ciccio's bad moods and even worse temper. He had listened to her beg for five minutes of her husband's attention. He had eventually grasped that the ideal goal composed of marriage, family and respectability could be a very expensive shrine to worship at. Had he not been made aware that it was his inherent duty to carry on the family line, nothing would have persuaded Vito into matrimony.

He studied the old car in the ditch with an amount of satisfaction that bemused him. It was a shabby ancient wreck of a vehicle. It had to mean that Holly was not a plant, not a spy or a member of the paparazzi, but a genuine traveller in trouble. Not that that reality softened his irritation over the fact that he was now stuck with her for at least one night. He had listened to the phone call she had made. Short of it being a matter of life or death, nobody was willing to come out on such a night. Of course he could have thrown his wealth at the problem to take care of it but nothing would more surely advertise his presence than the hiring of a helicopter to remove his unwanted guest, and he was doubtful that even a helicopter could fly in such poor conditions.

'As you see…it's stuck,' Holly pointed out unnecessarily while patting the bonnet of the car as if it were a live entity in need of comfort. 'It's my friend's car and she's going to be really upset about this.'

'Accidents happen…particularly if you choose to drive without taking precautions on a road like this in this kind of weather.'

In disbelief, Holly rounded on him, twin spots of high colour sparking over her cheekbones. 'It wasn't snowing this bad when I left home! There were no precautions!'

'Let's get your stuff and head back to the house.'

Suppressing the anger his tactless comment had roused with some difficulty, Holly studied him in astonishment. 'You're inviting me back to the house? You don't need to. I can—'

'I'm a notoriously unsympathetic man but even I could not leave you to sleep in a car in a snowstorm on Christmas Eve!' Vito framed impatiently. 'Now, may we cut the conversation and head back to the heat? Or do you want to pat the car again?'

Face red now with mortification, Holly opened the boot and dug out her rucksack to swing it up onto her back.

The rucksack was almost as big as she was, Vito saw in disbelief. 'Let me take that.'

'No...I was hoping you'd take the box because it's heavier.'

Stubborn mouth flattening, Vito reached in with reluctance for the sizeable box and hefted it up with a curled lip. 'Do you really need the box as well?'

'Yes, it's got all my stuff in it...*please*,' Holly urged.

Her amazingly blue eyes looked up at him and he felt strangely disorientated. Her eyes were as translucent a blue as the Delft masterpieces his mother had conserved from his grandfather's world-famous collection. They trudged back up the lane with Vito maintaining a disgruntled silence as he carried the bulky carton.

'*Porca miseria!* What's in the box?'

'My Christmas decorations and some food.'

'Why are you driving round with Christmas decorations and food? Of course, you were heading to a party,' he reasoned for himself, thinking of what she wore.

'No, I wasn't. I intended to spend the night with my foster mother because I thought she was going to be on her own for Christmas. *But*...turns out her son came and collected her and she didn't know I was planning to surprise her, so when I went off the road I was driving home again.'

'Where's home?'

She named a town Vito had never heard of.

'Where are you from?'

'Florence…in Italy,' he explained succinctly.

'I do know where Florence is…it *is* famous,' Holly countered, glancing up at him while the snow drifted down steadily, quietly, cocooning them in the small space lit by his torch. 'So, you're Italian.'

'You do like to state the obvious, don't you?' Vito derided, stomping into the porch one step behind her.

'I hate that sarcasm of yours!' Holly fired back at him angrily, taking herself almost as much by surprise as she took him because she usually went out of her way to avoid conflict.

An elegant black brow raised, Vito removed the boots, hung his coat and scarf and then lifted the rucksack from her bent shoulders. 'What have you got in here? Rocks?'

'Food.'

'The kitchen here is packed with food.'

'Do you always know better than everyone else about everything?' Holly, whose besetting fault was untidiness, carefully hung her wet coat beside his to be polite.

'I very often *do* know better,' Vito answered without hesitation.

Holly spread a shaken glance over his lean, darkly handsome and wholly serious features and groaned out loud. 'No sense of humour either.'

'Knowing one's own strengths is not a flaw,' Vito informed her gently.

'But it is if you don't consider your faults—'

'And what are *your* faults?' Vito enquired saccharine smooth, as she headed for the fire like a homing pigeon and held her hands out to the heat.

Holly wrinkled her snub nose and thought hard. 'I'm untidy. An incurable optimist. Too much of a people-pleaser... That comes of all those years in foster care and trying to fit in to different families and different schools.' She angled her head to one side, brown hair lying in a silken mass against one creamy cheek as she pondered. In the red Santa get-up, she reminded him of a cheerful little robin he had once seen pacing on a fence. 'I'm too forgiving sometimes because I always want to think the best of people or give them a second chance. I get really cross if I run out of coffee but I don't like conflict and avoid it. I like to do things quickly but sometimes that means I don't do them well. I fuss about my weight but I *still* don't exercise...'

As Vito listened to that very frank résumé he almost laughed. There was something intensely sweet about that forthright honesty. 'Strengths?' he prompted, unable to resist the temptation.

'I'm honest, loyal, hardworking, punctual...I like to make the people I care about happy,' she confided. 'That's what put me on that road tonight.'

'Would you like a drink?' Vito enquired.

'Red wine, if you have it...' Moving away from the fire, Holly approached her rucksack. 'Is it all right if I put the food in the kitchen?'

She walked through the door he indicated and her eyebrows soared along with the ceiling. Beyond that door the cottage changed again. A big extension housed an ultra-modern kitchen diner with pale sparkling gran-ite work surfaces and a fridge large enough to answer the storage needs of a restaurant. She opened it up. It was already generously packed with goodies, mainly of the luxury version of ready meals. She arranged her offerings on an empty shelf and then walked back into the main room to open the box and extract the food that remained.

Obviously, she was stuck here in a strange house with a strange man for one night at the very least, Holly reflected anxiously. A slight frisson of unease trickled down her spine. Vito hadn't done or said anything threatening, though, she reminded herself. Like her, he recognised practicalities. He was stuck with her because she had nowhere else to go and clearly he wasn't overjoyed by the situation. Neither one of them had a choice but to make the best of it.

'You brought a lot of food with you,' Vito remarked from behind her.

Holly flinched because she hadn't heard him approach and she whipped her head around. 'I assumed I would be providing a Christmas lunch for two people.'

Walking back out of the kitchen when she had finished, she found him frowning down at the tree ornaments visible in the box.

'What is all this stuff?' he asked incredulously.

Holly explained. 'Would it be all right if I put up my tree here? I mean, it is Christmas Eve and I won't get another opportunity for a year,' she pointed out. 'Christmas is special to me.'

Vito was still frowning. 'Not to me,' he admitted flatly, for he had only bad memories of the many disappointing Christmases he had endured as a child.

Flushing, Holly closed the box and pushed it over to the wall out of the way. 'That's not a problem. You're doing enough letting me stay here.'

Dio mio, he was relieved that she was only a passing stranger because her fondness for the sentimental trappings of the season set his teeth on edge. Of course she wanted to put up her Christmas tree! Anyone who travelled around wearing a Santa hat was likely to want a tree on display as well! He handed her a glass of wine, trying not to feel responsible for having doused her chirpy flow of chatter.

'I'm heading upstairs for a shower,' Vito told her, because even though he had worn the boots, his suit trousers were damp. 'Will you be all right down here on your own?'

'Of course... This is much better than sitting in a crashed car,' Holly assured him before adding more awkwardly, 'Do you have a sweater or anything I could borrow? I only have pyjamas and a dress with me. My foster mum's house is very warm so I didn't pack anything woolly.'

Vito had not a clue what was in his luggage because he hadn't packed his own case since he was a teenager at boarding school. 'I'll see what I've got.'

Through the glass barrier of the stairs, Holly watched his long, powerful legs disappear from view and a curious little frisson rippled through her tense body. She heaved a sigh. So, no Christmas tree. What possible objection could anyone have to a Christmas tree? Did Vito share Ebenezer Scrooge's loathing for the festive season? Reminding herself that she was *very* lucky not to be shivering in Pixie's car by the side of the road, she settled down on the shaggy rug by the hearth and simply luxuriated in the warmth emanating from the logs glowing in the fire.

Vito thought about Holly while he took a shower. It

was a major mistake. Within seconds of picturing her sexy little body he went hard as a rock, his body reacting with a randy enthusiasm that astonished him. For months, of course, his libido had very much taken a back seat to the eighteen-hour days he was working. This year the bank's revenues would, he reminded himself with pride, smash all previous records. He was doing what he had been raised to do and he was doing it extremely well, so why did he feel so empty, so joyless? Vito asked himself in exasperation.

Intellectually he understood that there was more to life than the pursuit of profit but realistically he was and always had been a workaholic. An image of Holly chattering by the fire assailed him. Holly with her wonderful curves and her weird tree in a box. She was unusual, not remotely like the sort of women Vito usually met, and her originality was a huge draw. He had no idea what she was likely to say next. She wasn't wearing make-up. She didn't fuss with her appearance. She said exactly what she thought and felt—she had no filter. Towelling off, he tried to stop thinking about Holly. Obviously she turned him on. Equally obviously he wasn't going to do anything about it.

Why the hell not? The words sounded in the back of his brain. That battered old car, everything about her spelled out the message that she came from a different world. Making any kind of a move would be taking advantage, he told himself grimly. Yet the instant he had seen Holly he had wanted her, *wanted* her with an intensity he hadn't felt around a woman since he was a careless teenager. It was the situation. He could relax with a woman who had neither a clue who he was nor any idea of the sleazy scandal currently clinging to his name. And why wouldn't he want her? After all, he was very probably sex-starved, he told himself impatiently as he tossed out the contents of one of his suitcases and then opened a second before finding a sweater he deemed suitable.

Holly watched Vito walk down the stairs with the fluid, silent grace of a panther. He had looked amazing in his elegant business suit, but in black designer jeans and a long-sleeved red cotton tee he was drop-dead gorgeous and, with those high cheekbones and that full masculine mouth, very much in the male-model category. She blinked and stared, feeling the colour rise in her cheeks, her self-consciousness taking over, for she had literally never ever been in the radius of such a very handsome male and it was just a little like bumping into a movie star without warning.

'Here… You can roll up the sleeves.' Vito tossed the sweater into her lap. 'If you want to freshen up, there's a shower room just before you enter the kitchen.'

Holly scrambled upright and grabbed her rucksack to take his advice. A little alone time to get her giddy head in order struck her as a very good idea. When she saw herself in the mirror in the shower room she was affronted by the wind-tousled explosion of her hair and the amount of cleavage she was showing in the Santa outfit. Stripping off, she went for a shower, exulting in the hot water and the famous-name shower gel on offer. Whoever owned the cottage had to be pretty comfortably off, she decided with a grimace, which probably meant that Vito was as well. He wore a very sleek gold-coloured watch and the fit of his suit had been perfection. But then what did she know about such trappings or the likely cost of them? Pixie would laugh to hear such musings when the closest Holly had ever got to even dating an office worker was Ritchie, the cheating insurance salesman.

She pulled on the blue sweater, which plunged low enough at the neck to reveal her bra. She yanked it at the back to raise it to a decent level at the front and knew she would have to remember to keep her shoulders back. She rolled up the sleeves and, since the sweater covered her to her knees, left off her tights. Her hair she rescued with a little diligent primping until it fell in loose waves round her shoulders. Frowning at her bunny slippers, she crammed them back in her rucksack, deciding that bare feet were preferable. Cosmetics-wise she was pretty much stuck with the minimal make-up she had packed for Sylvia's. Sighing, she used tinted moisturiser, subtle eyeliner and glossed her lips. Well, at short notice that was the best she could do. In any case it was only her pride that was prompting her to make the effort. After all, a male as sophisticated as Vito Sorrentino wouldn't look at her anyway, she thought with a squirming pang of guilty disappointment. Why on earth was she thinking about him that way?

And thinking about Vito that way put her back in mind of Ritchie, which was unfortunate. But it also reminded her that she hadn't taken her pill yet and she dug into her bag to remedy that, only to discover that she had left them at home. As to why a virgin was taking contraceptive precautions, she and Pixie both did on a 'better safe than sorry' basis. Both of their mothers had messed up their lives with early unplanned pregnancies and neither Holly nor Pixie wanted to run the same risk.

Of course a couple of years back Holly had had different and more romantic expectations. She had fondly imagined that she would eventually meet a man who would sweep her away on a tide of passion and she had believed that she had to protect herself in the face of such temptation. Sadly, nothing any boyfriend had yet made her feel could have fallen into a category that qualified as being *swept away*. Since then Holly had wondered if there was a distinct possibility that she herself simply wasn't a very passionate woman. Still, Holly reasoned wryly, there was nothing wrong with living in hope, was there?

Somehow Vito had been fully expecting Holly to reappear with a full face of make-up. Instead she appeared with her face rosy and apparently untouched, his sweater drooping round her in shapeless, bulky folds, her tiny feet bare. And Vito almost laughed out loud in appreciation and relief. What remained of his innate wariness was evaporating fast because no woman he had ever yet met could possibly have put less effort into trying to attract him than Holly. Before his engagement and even since it he had been targeted so often by predatory women that he had learned to be guarded in his behaviour around females, both inside and outside working hours. His rare smile flashed across his lean, strong face.

Holly collided involuntarily with molten gold eyes enhanced by thick black lashes and then that truly heart-stopping smile that illuminated his darkly handsome features, and her heart not only bounced in her chest but also skipped an entire beat in reaction. She came to an abrupt halt, her fingers dropping from her ruck-sack. 'Do you want me to make something to eat?' she offered shakily, struggling to catch her breath.

'No, thanks. I ate before you arrived,' Vito drawled

lazily, watching her shrug back the sweater so that it didn't slip too low at the front. No, she really *wasn't* trying to pull him and he was captivated as he so rarely was by a woman.

'Then you won't mind if *I* eat? I brought supper with me,' she explained, moving past him towards the kitchen.

She's not even going to try to entertain me, Vito reflected, positively rapt in admiration in receipt of that clear demonstration of indifference.

When had he become so arrogant that he expected every young woman he came into contact with to make a fuss of him and a play for him?

It wasn't arrogance, he reasoned squarely. He was as rich as Midas and well aware that that was the main reason for his universal appeal. He poured Holly a fresh glass of wine and carried it into the kitchen for her. She closed the oven, wool stretching to softly define her heart-shaped derrière.

'Do you have a boyfriend?' he heard himself enquire, seemingly before his brain had formed the question, while his attention was still lodged on the sweater that both concealed and revealed her lush curves.

'No. As of today I have an ex,' Holly told him. 'You?'

'I'm single.' Vito lounged back against the kitchen island, the fine fabric of his pants pulling taut to define long, muscular thighs *and*…the noticeable masculine bulge at his crotch. Heat surging into her cheeks, Holly dragged her straying attention off him and stared down at her wine. Since when had she looked at a man *there*? Her breath was snarled up in her throat and her entire body felt super sensitive.

'What happened today?' Vito probed.

'I caught Ritchie having sex with his receptionist on his lunch break,' Holly told him in a rush before she could think better of that humiliating admission. Unfortunately looking at Vito had wrecked her composure to such an extent that she barely knew what she was saying any more.

CHAPTER THREE

IN RECEIPT OF that startling confession, Vito had the most
atrocious desire to laugh, but he didn't want to hurt
Holly's feelings. Her cheeks had gone all pink again and
her eyes were evasive as if that confession had simply
slipped accidentally from her lips. He breathed in deep.
'Tough. What did you do?'

'Told him what I thought of him in one sentence,
walked out again.' Holly tilted her chin, anger darken-
ing her blue eyes as she remembered the scene she had
interrupted. 'I hate liars and cheats.'

'I'm shockingly well behaved in that line. Too busy
working,' Vito countered, relieved that she had not a
clue about the scandal that had persuaded him to leave
Florence and even less idea of who he was. In recent
days he had been forced to spend way too much time
in the company of people too polite to say what they
thought but not too polite to stare at him and whisper.
Anonymity suddenly had huge appeal. He finally felt
that he could relax.

'So, why are you staying here all alone?' Holly asked,
sipping her wine, grateful he had glossed over her gaffe
about Ritchie without further comment.

'Burnout. I needed a break from work.' Vito gave

her the explanation he had already decided on in the shower. 'Obviously I wasn't expecting weather like this.'

He was unusually abstracted, however, ensnared by the manner in which the blue of his sweater lit up her luminous eyes. He was also wondering how she could possibly look almost irresistibly cute in an article of his clothing when the thick wool draped her tiny body like a blanket and only occasionally hinted at the treasures that lay beneath. What was the real secret of her appeal? he was asking himself in bewilderment, even though the secret was right in front of him. She had a wonderfully feminine shape, amazing eyes and a torrent of dark hair that tumbled round her shoulders in luxuriant loose curls. But what was most different about Holly was that she was genuine as so few people dared to be. She put on no show and said nothing for effect; indeed she followed a brand of candour that was blunt to the point of embarrassing.

'Why are you staring at me?' Holly asked baldly, straightening her spine and squaring her little shoulders for all the world as though she was bracing herself for him to say something critical.

'Am I?' Vito fielded, riveting dark eyes brimming with amusement as he straightened to leave the kitchen. 'Sorry... I didn't mean to make you uncomfortable.'

He was setting up a games console when Holly joined him with her plate of savoury snacks. 'I thought I'd have a game,' he told her, 'but perhaps you would rather watch TV—'

'No, what game is it?'

It was a war game Holly knew well. 'I'll play you,' she told him.

Vito shot her a startled glance. 'You play?'

'Of course I do. Every foster family had a console and you learned to play with the other kids to fit in,' she pointed out wryly.

'*Dio mio*...how many different families did you live with?'

'I never counted but there were a lot of them. I'd get settled somewhere and then someone somewhere would decide I should have another go at bonding with my mother, and I'd be shot back to her again for a few months.'

Vito was frowning as he set up the game. 'Your mother was still alive?'

'Just not a good parent. It never worked out with her,' Holly completed wryly, keen to gloss over the facts with as little detail as possible while she watched Vito, lean hips flexing down into powerful thighs as he bent down.

From her position kneeling on the floor, she could admire the fluidity of his long-fingered brown hands as he leant over the console. His every movement was incredibly graceful, she acknowledged. And when she glanced up at him she noticed the black density of his eyelashes and the definition that dark luxuriance lent to his already stunning dark eyes. Her nipples were tight little buds inside her bra and she felt hot.

'Your father?' Vito queried.

'I had no idea who my father was so he didn't come into the picture. But my mother still being around was the reason why I moved around so much, because she refused to allow me to be put up for adoption. Every time I went back to my mother and then had to leave her again to go back into care, I ended up with a new foster family.' Holly grimaced and shrugged. 'It was a messy way to grow up.'

Vito had always thought he had it rough with a tyrannical grandfather, warring parents and being an only child on whom huge expectations rested. But his glimpse at what lay on Holly's side of the fence sobered him and gave him an unsettling new perspective. He had always had security and he had always known he was loved. And although Holly had enjoyed neither advantage, she wasn't moaning about it, he thought with grudging appreciation.

As Vito lounged back on the sofa his six-pack abs rippled below the soft cotton stretched over his broad chest and Holly's mouth ran dry. He was amazingly beautifully built and the acknowledgement sent colour surging into her cheeks because she had never looked at a man's body and thought that before. But she couldn't take her eyes off him and it mortified her. It was as if she had been locked back into a teenager's body again because there was nothing sensible or controlled about what she was experiencing.

'We'll set the timer for a ten-minute challenge,' Vito told her lightly, doubting that she would last the game that long.

Fortunately, Holly didn't even have to think while she played him. In dark times the engrossing, mindless games had been her escape from the reality of a life that hurt too much. With the weapon she had picked she made kill after kill on screen and then the challenge was over and she had won.

'You're very fast,' Vito conceded with a slashing grin of appreciation, because once again he could not think of a single woman who, having chosen to play him, would not have then allowed him to win even though she was a better player. Of course that was a debatable point when he didn't actually know any other woman who could play.

'Lots of practice over the years,' Holly conceded, still recovering from the raw charisma of that wolfish grin that cracked right through his essential reserve. Gaming had relaxed him, warmed him up, melted that cool façade he wore to show the real man underneath. And now he didn't just strike her as heartbreakingly handsome, he was downright irresistible. She shifted uneasily in her seat, her body tense and so weirdly super sensitive that even her clothes seemed to chafe her tender skin.

'And the prize is…' Vito's attention locked like a missile to the soft pink fullness of her mouth and her nipples pinched into tight little points. 'You get to put your Christmas tree up.'

Holly sprang off the seat. 'Seriously?' she exclaimed in surprise.

'Seriously.' Vito focused on that sparkling smile and gritted his teeth in a conscious attempt to cool off and quell his hard-on. He didn't know what it was about her but one look from those melting blue eyes and he was hotter than hell. 'Go ahead…' He pinched one of the snacks on her plate by his feet. 'Any more of these?'

Holly laughed. 'I'll put more on before I get the tree sorted.'

Vito watched her rush about full of energy, and sup-pressed a rueful sigh. It didn't take a lot to make her happy. 'Why does Christmas mean so much to you?'

'I didn't have it when I was very small,' she admitted.

'How can you *not* have Christmas?'

'Mum didn't celebrate it. Well, not in the family sense. There was no tree, no present, nothing. She went

out partying but I didn't know what the day was supposed to be until I went into care for the first time.'

Vito frowned. 'And how did that happen?'

Holly hesitated, eyes troubled as her oval face stiffened. 'You know, this is all very personal...'

'I'm curious...I've never met anyone who grew up
in care before,' Vito told her truthfully, revelling in
every fleeting expression that crossed her expressive
little face. She was full to the brim with emotional responses. She was his exact opposite because she felt
so much and showed even more. It shook him that he
could find that ingenuousness so very appealing in a
woman that he was challenged to look away from her.

Holly compressed her lips, those full pink lips with
that dainty little cupid's bow that called to him on a far
more primitive level. 'When I was six years old, Mum
left me alone for three days over Christmas. I went to
a neighbour because I was hungry and she called the
police.'

Taken aback by that admission, Vito sat up very
straight, dark-as-night eyes locked to her as she finished
that little speech in an emotive surge. 'Your mother
abandoned you?'

'Yes, but eventually she probably would have come
back, as she'd done it before. I was put into a short-term
foster home and the family gave me Christmas even
though it was already over,' Holly told him with a fond
smile of remembrance.

'And you've been making up for that loss ever since,'
Vito said drily, shrugging off the pangs of sympathy
assailing him, taking refuge in edgy cynicism instead.
He didn't do emotion, avoiding such displays and feelings whenever he could because the memories of his

mother's raw pain in the face of his father's rejections still disturbed him. As far as he was concerned, if you put your feelings out on display you were asking to be kicked in the teeth and it was not a risk he was prepared to take for anyone. Yet just looking at Holly he could tell that she had taken that same risk time and time again.

'Probably. As obsessions go, Christmas is a fairly harmless one,' Holly fielded before she got up to hurry into the kitchen and retrieve the snacks from the oven. After handing him the plate, she returned to winding the fairy lights round the small tree.

He watched the firelight flicker over her, illuminating a rounded cheekbone, a tempting stretch of gleaming thigh as she bent down, and the provocative rise of her curvy behind. 'How old are you, Holly?'

Holly attached an ornament to a branch and glanced over her shoulder at him. As soon as she collided with his spellbinding dark golden eyes, her heart raced, her mouth ran dry and her mind went blank. 'I'm twenty-four...tomorrow.'

Vito's gaze glittered in the firelight. 'It's both Christmas *and* your birthday.'

'Now it's your turn. Tell me about you,' Holly urged with unconcealed eagerness because everything about Vito Sorrentino made her insanely curious.

It should not have been an unexpected question but it hit Vito like a brick and he froze on the reality that having questioned her so thoroughly he could hardly refuse to respond in kind. He breathed in deep, squaring his broad shoulders, fighting his tension. 'I'm the only child of ill-matched parents. Holiday periods when my father was expected to play his part as a family man were always very stressful because he hated being forced to spend time with us. Christmas fell into that category.'

'Why haven't they separated?' He was so on edge talking about his family situation that it touched her heart. Such a beautiful man, so sophisticated and cool in comparison to her, so seemingly together and yet he too bore the damage of a wounding childhood. Holly was fascinated.

'My mother was raised to believe that divorce is wrong...and she loves my father. She's incredibly loyal to the people she loves.' Vito spoke very stiffly because he had never in his life before shared that much about his family dynamics. He had been taught to live by the same code of secretive silence and polite denial that his mother had always observed. Even if the roof was falling in, appearances still had to be conserved. Breaking that code of silence with an outsider filled him with discomfiture.

'That must've put a lot of pressure on you,' Holly remarked, soulful big blue eyes pinned to him with an amount of sympathy far beyond what he considered necessary.

And yet inexplicably there was something in Vito that was warmed by that show of support. He came up off the sofa as though she had yanked a chain attached to his body, and pulled her up into his arms, and in neither of those moves did he recognise conscious thought or decision. It was instinct, pure instinct to reach for Holly.

He tugged her close, long brown fingers flying up to tilt her chin, and gazed down into those inviting clear eyes of hers. A split second later, he kissed her.

In shock, Holly simply stood there, conflicting feelings pulling her in opposing directions. *Push him away, back off* now, one voice urged. *He finds me attractive, find out what it's like*, the other voice pleaded while she brimmed with secret pride. He touched her mouth slow and soft, nipping her lips lightly and teasingly, and she could hardly breathe. Her heart was thumping like a jackhammer inside her ribcage. His tongue eased apart the seam of her lips and flickered and a spasm of raw excitement thrilled down into her pelvis. With a hungry groan he tightened his arms round her.

Nothing had ever tasted as good as Vito's mouth on hers and she trembled in reaction, her whole body awakening. Her hands linked round his neck as the hard, demanding pressure of his mouth sent a delicious heat spiralling down through her. She felt wonderfully warm and safe for the first time ever. In that moment of security she rejoiced in the glorious feel of his mouth and the taste of the wine on his tongue. His fingers splayed to mould to her hips and trailed down the backs of her thighs. Tiny little shivers of response tugged at her as she felt a tightening sensation at her core and her breasts felt achingly full.

Vito lifted his dark head. Dark golden eyes sought hers. 'I want you,' he husked.

'I want you,' Holly framed shakily and it was the very first time she understood the need to say that to someone.

In all the years she had thought about having sex it had always been because sex was expected of her in a relationship, never because she herself was tempted. In the face of those expectations, her body had begun to seem like something to cede, and not fully her own. And that had been wrong, *so* wrong, she finally saw. It should be her choice and her choice alone. But she was learning that only now in Vito's arms and recognising the difference because she was finally experiencing a genuine desire for something more. And it was a heady feeling that left her bemused and giddy.

Staring up into Vito's dark, dangerous eyes, she stretched up on tiptoe to reach him, simply desperate to feel his beautiful mouth on hers again. And the sheer strength of that physical connection, the locking in of every simultaneous sensation that assailed her, only emphasised how right it felt to be with him that way.

This was what all the fuss was about, she thought joyously, the thrumming pulse of need that drove her, the tiny little tremors of desire making her tremble, the overwhelming yearning for the hard, muscular feel of his body against hers. And as one kiss led into another he drew her down onto the rug again and the heat of the fire on her skin burned no more fiercely than the raw hunger raging through her with spellbinding force.

With her willing collusion he extracted her from the sweater and released the catch on her bra. He studied the full globes he had bared with unhidden hunger. 'You have a totally amazing body, *gioia mia*.'

A deep flush lit Holly's cheeks and the colour spread because she was not relaxed about nudity. Yet there in the firelight with Vito looking at her as though he were unveiling a work of art, she was horribly self-conscious but she felt no shame or sense of inadequacy. Indeed, the more Vito looked, the more the pulse of heat humming between her thighs picked up tempo. Long fingers shaping the plump curves of her breasts, Vito flicked a tongue over a straining pink nipple and a hungry groan of appreciation was wrenched from him as he dallied there, toying with her sensitive flesh in a caress that made her hips squirm while a new sense of urgency gripped her.

'Kiss me,' she urged breathlessly as he tugged at the tender buds of her breasts and an arrow of burning heat pierced her feminine core, only increasing her agitation.

He crushed her ripe mouth beneath his again, his tongue plunging deep, and for a split second it satisfied the craving pulling at her, and then somehow even that wasn't enough any more. She shifted position restively, her legs sliding apart to let his hips slide between as she silently, instinctively sought more. Her hips rocked. She wanted and she *wanted*…

And then at last, as if he knew exactly what she needed, he smoothed his passage up a silken inner thigh and tugged off her panties. He stroked her, found the most needy place of all, and a current of almost unbearable excitement shot through Holly's veins. Suddenly in the hold of her own explosive response she was all heat and light and sensation. A long finger tested her slick, damp core and she whimpered, her teeth clenching, the ferocious need clawing cruelly at her as her spine arched, her body all too ready to take charge.

There was no room for thought in the passion that had swept her away in the way she had always dreamed. But it wasn't the same as her dream because what she was feeling was much more basic, much more wild and out of control than she had ever allowed herself to be. He moved to one side, yanking off his top, revealing an abdomen grooved with lean, hard muscle, and her hand slid greedily up over his chest, rejoicing in his sleek bronzed skin and the manner in which every muscle jerked taut the instant she touched him.

'I have no condoms,' Vito bit out in sudden frustration. 'But I had a health check a few weeks ago and I'm clean.'

'I'm on the pill,' Holly framed shakily, belatedly jolted into rational thought by the acknowledgement that she wasn't about to call a halt to their activities. And why was that? She had never wanted anything or anyone the way she wanted him and surely that was the way it was supposed to be? It felt right. *He* felt right.

Vito hauled in a shuddering breath of relief and came back down to her again, tasting her reddened mouth again with devouring appetite. Her hands smoothed over him, caressing every part of him she could reach from his wide brown shoulders to the satin-smooth expanse of his back. Desire drove her like an addictive drug. Beneath his touch she writhed, her reactions pitching her desire higher and higher until the mushroom of liquid-honey heat inside her flared up in ecstasy before spreading to every part of her. She gasped, shaken by an almost out-of-body feeling, her entire being singing with the potent rush of pleasure.

And then she felt him pushing at the heart of her, tilting her back for his entrance and she was wildly impatient, needing more, ready to try anything that he could give her. He filled her completely, thrusting deep with a slick, sure forcefulness that took her by surprise. The bite of pain was an equal surprise and she blinked back tears and sank her teeth into her lower lip, grateful that her face was against his shoulder where he couldn't see her reaction.

'You're incredibly wet and tight,' Vito growled in a roughened undertone. 'It's a hell of a turn-on, *gioia mia*.'

The pinch of discomfort evaporated as he moved

and she arched up to receive him. He vented a groan of all-male satisfaction as she joined in, no longer separate in thought and behaviour. That overpowering hunger kicked back in as his fluid, insistent thrusts filled her with renewed enthusiasm. In fact the wild, sweet rhythm of his sensual possession fired a blinding, pulsing excitement inside her. Locked with his, her body was snatched up into a passionate climax that flooded her with exquisite sensation.

Coiling back from her, Vito saw the blood on her thighs. '*Maledizione*...you're bleeding? Did I hurt you? Why didn't you stop me?'

Brutally summoned back to reality without warning, Holly snaked back from him and hugged her knees in sudden mortification. 'It's all right—'

'No, you being hurt is *not* all right in any way,' Vito shot back at her grimly.

Holly could feel a beetroot-red flush start at her toes and slowly burn up over her whole body. Lifting her head, she clashed reluctantly with glittering dark eyes of angry concern. 'I wasn't hurt...at least not the way you mean,' she explained grudgingly. 'I was a virgin... and obviously there was some physical evidence of it... which I wasn't expecting...'

'A virgin?' Vito exclaimed in raw disbelief. 'You were a *virgin*?'

Snatching up the sweater he had taken off her, Holly pulled it over her again, struggling to slide her arms back into the sleeves. 'Don't make such a big deal of it,' she urged while she was still safely submerged in the wool.

'It *is* a big deal!' Vito grated, springing upright to zip his trousers again and reach for his shirt.

Flushed and uncomfortable, Holly glanced at him

unwillingly. 'Maybe to me but I don't see why it should bother you!'

'Don't you indeed?' Vito riposted.

'No, I don't,' Holly countered on a rising note of anger because his reaction was the very last thing she had expected from him and the topic mortified her.

Dark eyes flashing gold, Vito studied her. 'You should've warned me. Why didn't you?'

Holly stood her ground, her vexation stifling her embarrassment. 'Because it was a private matter and none of your business.'

'Nothing of that nature stays private when you're having sex with someone!'

In discomfited retreat, Holly headed towards the shower room she had used earlier. 'Well, I'll take your word for that since it was my first experience.'

Vito was inflamed by her refusal to understand and chose to be blunt. 'I feel like I took advantage of you!' he admitted harshly.

Holly whirled back at the door. 'That's nonsense. I'm not a kid. My body, my choice.'

Vito snatched in a ragged breath, still reeling from the shock of her innocence. He hadn't told her who he was or indeed anything important about himself. She didn't, *couldn't* understand that in his position he was innately suspicious of anything as unexpected as their encounter and on top of it the very tardy revelation that she was a virgin. With his experience, that revelation had smacked of a possible sting of some kind and he had immediately wondered if she had some kind of hidden agenda. Now gazing into her troubled face, belatedly recognising the hurt and sadness there, he wanted to kick himself for treating her like some sort of scam artist.

'I'm sorry...' Vito breathed abruptly. 'I let my surprise push me into an overreaction, Holly. Of course, it's your choice...'

Some of her tension evaporated but her eyes remained guarded. 'I didn't even think of warning you. And if I *had* thought of it, I probably would've been too embarrassed to mention it.'

'I wrecked the moment,' Vito groaned in acknowledgement. He moved forward to close his arms round her and somehow, even after that uneasy exchange, it felt like the best thing in the world to Holly. Her stiffness slowly ebbing, she rested against him, drinking in the heat and the comfortingly hard, masculine contours of his lean, muscular body against hers. 'I also neglected to tell you that what we shared...it was amazing.'

'You're just saying that,' she mumbled.

'No. It *was* amazing, *cara mia*. Now let's go upstairs and shower,' Vito urged, easing her in a different direction, inexplicably keen to keep her close even though something in his brain was urging him to step back.

Amazing? Was that a polite lie? Just something a man said for the sake of it? He had flipped the situation on its head again and she didn't know how he had achieved that. She blinked in surprise as the lights illuminated a much bigger bedroom than she had expected, airily furnished in stylish tones of grey.

Vito pushed open the door of a very spacious en-suite. 'You first...unless you'd like company in the shower?'

Holly gave him a startled look. 'I don't think I'm ready for that yet.'

Vito laughed in appreciation and bent down to claim her swollen pink mouth with his own in a searing kiss that made every skin cell in her body sit up and take notice. 'I'll ask you again in the morning,' he warned her.

Holly's attention skated to the giant bed. 'We're going to share the bed?'

'There is only one bedroom here. I was planning to take the sofa.'

'No, I won't banish you to the sofa,' Holly breathed with a sudden grin as she slid past him into the en-suite while barely recognising her own thoughts or feelings. She only knew she didn't want him to sleep downstairs on the sofa and away from her. That felt wrong.

She stood in the shower feeling astonishingly light-hearted for a woman who had strayed from values that were as ingrained in her as her usual honesty. But making love with Vito had felt right and it was hard to credit that anything that had felt so natural and right could possibly be wrong. After all, they were both single and nobody was being hurt by their being together. What harm could it possibly do for her to go with the flow for a change in a relationship instead of trying to plan everything or wait for some extraordinary special sign? And why on earth was she feeling guilty about Ritchie when *he* had cheated on *her*?

It wasn't as though she had ever imagined that she was in love with Ritchie. She had only been seeing him for a few weeks and, even though he had been full of himself, he had been good company. Was what she felt with Vito a rebound attraction?

But how could it be? Ritchie couldn't be compared to Vito on any level. Vito utterly overshadowed his predecessor in every way. And just like her secret fantasy,

Vito had swept Holly away in the tide of passion she had always dreamt of experiencing. Of course, it wasn't going anywhere, she reminded herself staunchly, suppressing a pang of sorrow at that acknowledgement. There would be no ongoing relationship with Vito. She didn't need Vito to spell that out. What they had now was time out of time, separate from their normal lives and associations. Attraction had sparked purely because they were stuck together in a snowbound cottage, and she wasn't foolish enough to try and make more of it, was she?

She wrapped a towel round herself rather than put on his sweater again and crept out of the bathroom. Clad only in his jeans, which were unbuttoned at the waistband, Vito was towelling his hair dry. He tossed aside the towel, finger-combing his black hair carelessly off his brow. 'I used the shower downstairs.'

Holly hovered, suddenly awkward. 'I could have done that. This is your room, after all.'

Vito saw the wary uncertainty in her blue eyes and knew he had put it there. Holly was nothing at all like the women he was accustomed to meeting. Nevertheless he had initially judged her by the cynical standards formed by years of experience with such women. Yet he sensed that she would have been very shocked by the scandal that he had been forced to leave behind him. He had wounded her by questioning her innocence yet that same innocence of hers ironically drew him like a beacon. He crossed the room and closed both arms round her, responding to the inbuilt drive to bridge the gap between them. 'Tonight it's *our* room. Let's go to bed...' he urged.

And Holly thought about saying no and heading

down to the sofa. After all, she had broken her own rules and just because she had done that once didn't mean she had an automatic excuse to keep on doing it. Indeed, if having sex with Vito had been a mistake, she was honour-bound to choose the sofa over him.

But sleeping alone wasn't what she wanted and needed right then. She wanted to be with Vito. She wanted to make the most of the time they had together. She was even feeling sensible enough to know that it was fortunate that she wouldn't be with Vito for much longer, for she reckoned that given the opportunity she would fall for him like a ton of bricks. That, of course, would be totally, unforgivably stupid. And she might be a little sentimental, but stupid she was not.

She looked at Vito, even though she knew she really shouldn't, but there he was, etched in her head in an image that would burn for all time, she thought dizzily. He was beautiful, drop-dead beautiful and tonight…tonight he was all *hers*…

CHAPTER FOUR

AT DAWN, HOLLY sneaked out of bed and crept into the bathroom to freshen up. She grimaced at her reflection. Her hair was a mess. Her face reddened in places by Vito's stubble. Her mouth was very swollen and pink. And when she stepped into the shower she swallowed a groan because every muscle she possessed complained as if she had overdone it in a workout.

But no workout, she thought dizzily, could possibly have been more demanding than the stamina required for a night in bed with Vito Sorrentino. He was insatiable and he had made her the same way, she conceded in stupefaction. She felt as though she had changed dramatically in less than twelve hours. She had learned so much about herself and even more about sex. Her body ached in intimate places and a bemused smile tilted her lips as she emerged from the en-suite again.

Vito was sprawled across the bed, a glorious display of bronzed perfection. Luxuriant black lashes flickered as he focused on her. 'I wondered where you were,' he muttered.

'Bathroom,' she whispered, barely breathing as she slid back under the duvet.

Vito reached for her with a sleepy hand and pulled

her back against him. She shivered in contact with the raw heat and scent of him. 'Go back to sleep,' he told her thickly.

He wanted her again. What the hell was wrong with him? How could he want her again when he had already had her so many times? She had to be sore too, he reminded himself in exasperation. He was being a selfish bastard. As soon as he heard the deep, even tenor of her breathing sink into sleep, he eased out of the bed, went for a cold shower and got dressed.

Nothing in Vito's mental rule book covered what had happened the night before. He hadn't had a one-night stand in many years and none had been extraordinary on any level. Sex was sex, a temporary release and pleasure. He was practical about sex, cool about sex. His desire had never controlled him and he would never let it do so. But then he had never ever been intimate with a woman he wanted over and over again, and his voracious hunger for Holly even after having her downright unnerved him. What was wrong with him? Was he in some weird frame of mind after the trying ordeal of the publicity fallout he had endured over the past week? In his opinion it certainly wasn't normal to want a woman *that* much. It smacked of unbalance, of unhealthy obsession. It was fortunate that their time together had a built-in closing date, he told himself grimly.

Even so, it was Christmas Day as well as being Holly's birthday and it bothered him that he had nothing to give her. Vito was so accustomed to gift-giving and other people's high expectations of his gifts that he felt very uncomfortable in that situation. In an effort to make the day special for Holly he decided to make her breakfast in bed. He couldn't cook but how difficult could it be to make breakfast? He could manage orange juice and toast, couldn't he?

Holly was stunned when she blinked into drowsy wakefulness because Vito was sliding a tray of food on to her lap. She stared down in wonderment at the charred toast. 'You made me breakfast?'

'It's your birthday. It's not much but it's the best I can do.'

Holly tried not to look at him as though he were the eighth wonder of the world but that was certainly how he struck her at that moment because nobody had ever given Holly breakfast in bed before, no, not even when she was ill. It was a luxury she could barely even imagine and that Vito should have gone to that much effort to spoil her thrilled her. So, she didn't make a sound when her first sip of tea gave her a mouthful of the teabag that had not been removed and she munched through the charred toast without complaint. It was the thought that counted, after all, and that Vito *had* thought touched her heart. In addition, the effect of having Vito carelessly sprawled at the foot of the same bed sent her pulse rate rocketing. She remembered all the things they had done and tried desperately to feel guilty about them. But it didn't work. One look into those inky-black-lashed dark golden eyes of his and she was shot off to another planet.

'Thanks,' she said even though it took great effort to locate her voice.

'I'm not great in the kitchen. If it had only been for me I would have cooked one of the ready meals,' he admitted.

'It was very thoughtful of you.' Holly was registering how very lucky she was not to be facing roast meat for breakfast and she gratefully drank her orange juice, which was so cold it froze her teeth. As she drained the glass she pushed the tray away and he swept it up and put it on the floor.

He came back to the bed and moved towards her with the sinuous grace of a stalking cat and her mouth ran dry, her heartbeat racing. 'I was going to get up, organise lunch,' she framed shakily.

'Way too early for that, *bellezza mia*,' Vito husked, up close, his breath fanning her cheek and his luxuriant black hair brushing her chin as he bent his head to press his mouth to the pulse point below her ear.

And her whole body went into free fall as though he had hit a button. Breath fled her parted lips as she sank back into the pillows and gazed up at him with luminous blue eyes. 'Vito—'

He closed her mouth with the onslaught of his own. 'No, we don't talk,' he told her after kissing her breathless. 'We already know all we need to know about each other.'

'I don't even know what you do,' she began.

'I'm in business...and you?'

'Waitress...well, waitress with aspirations,' she adjusted jerkily when he tensed against her. 'I want to be an interior designer but it's more a dream than reality.'

'It takes work to turn dreams into reality.'

Holly smiled up at him. 'Vito... I've had to work hard for everything in life but sometimes getting a break relates more to resources and luck than slaving away.'

'This is getting way too serious,' Vito objected when he found himself on the brink of offering her advice.

Holly let her fingers drift up to brush his black hair off his brow, her attention locked to his lean, darkly handsome features even as her heart had sunk because she was scarily well attuned to his body language. 'Agreed. Let's stay away from the real world.'

His long, lean body relaxed against hers again and tears stung her eyes as she blinked against his shoulder. The news that she was a waitress had been too sharp a stab of reality for Vito, highlighting as it did the difference in their statuses. His clothing, even the variety and expense of the food in the refrigerator, not to mention the stylish opulence of her surroundings all told Holly that Vito inhabited a rather more privileged place in society than she did. And while here at the cottage without other people around, that difference didn't really matter. She knew it would matter very much outside these walls.

'I still want you,' Vito confided thickly, running the tip of his tongue along her collarbone.

Her tummy flipped, her feminine core clenched and she stiffened. Reality was intruding whether she wanted it to or not because she was too tender to engage again in the kind of intimacy he was probably envisaging. 'I can't,' she whispered tightly, a small hand smoothing down a denim-clad thigh, feeling the ripple of his muscles tightening in response.

'Maybe later,' Vito murmured sibilantly, fingers spearing into her hair to lift her mouth to his. 'But in the short term there are other things we can do, *gioia mia*.'

Holly laughed and buried her face in his shoulder. 'You're so shameless.'

'Why wouldn't I be? You've been brilliant. I can't understand why you were still untouched.'

'It was a promise I made to myself when I was very young...to wait. It just seemed sensible to wait until I was an adult and then...' Holly sighed. 'Somewhere along the line it became a burden, a tripwire in relation-ships that held me back from who I could be.'

Vito gazed down at her with a frown of incompre-hension. 'But why me? Why did you choose me?'

'Maybe it was because you let me put my Christmas tree up,' she teased, because there were all too many reasons why she had chosen him and very few she was prepared to share. There was no safe way to tell a man that he had been her fantasy without him getting the wrong idea and assuming that she was feeling more than she was supposed to feel in terms of attachment.

Her fingers slid up caressingly to the firm bulge at his crotch and exerted gentle pressure and he groaned, dark head falling back, wide sensual mouth tightening, his broad chest vibrating against her. Holly leant over him, staring down into lustrous eyes that glittered like precious gold. 'Maybe it's because you act as though I'm the most ravishing female you've ever met, even though I'm perfectly ordinary. But perhaps that's your true talent. Maybe you treat all women the same way.'

'No. I've never been with any woman the way I've been with you...' Vito surveyed her with frowning force, probing that statement, worrying about it because it was true. He had never felt so comfortable with a woman or so relaxed. He hadn't once thought about work or about the shocking scandal he had left behind him in Italy. Furthermore Holly was completely unique on his terms because for the first time ever he was with a woman who didn't know who he was, cherished no financial expectations and in truth attached no undue importance to him. He was Mr Anonymous with Holly and he liked the freedom of that one hell of a lot.

Holly unzipped his jeans with a sense of adventure.

Her most driving need was to give him pleasure and she didn't understand it. Shouldn't she be more selfish? The catch in his breathing was followed by a long, unrestrained sound of rising hunger. She had distracted him with sex, she thought guiltily. She didn't want to talk about being a waitress, about any of the things that separated them as people in the outside world, and his unashamed sexual response to her gave her a shocking sense of power.

Heaven for Vito was the gentle friction of her mouth and the teasing, erotic stroke of her tiny fingers. His hand knotted in her hair and he trembled on the edge of release, gruffly warning her, but she didn't pull away. Then the sheer liberating wash of pleasure engulfed him and wiped him out.

Holly watched Vito sleep with a rueful grin. She went for another shower, donned the dress she had packed and dried her hair. Downstairs, she switched on the television and tuned it to a channel playing Christmas carols before going into the kitchen and beginning to organise the lunch she had prepared with such care. It shook her to acknowledge that she hadn't even known Vito Sorrentino existed the day before.

The shame and embarrassment she had fought off at dawn began to creep up again through the cracks in her composure. She had broken all her rules and for what? A one-night stand with a male she would probably never hear from or see again? How could she be proud of that? But would it have been any better to lose her virginity with a sleazy, cheating liar like Ritchie, who had pretended that she meant much more to him than she did?

She thought not. Anyway, it was too late for regrets, she reminded herself unhappily. What was done was done and it made more sense to move on from that point than to torture herself over what could not be changed. How much, though, had all the wine she had imbibed contributed to her recklessness? Her loss of inhibition? *Stop it, stop it*, she urged herself fiercely, *stop dwelling on it.*

Vito came down the stairs when she was setting the table. 'You should have wakened me.'

'You were up much earlier than I was,' she pointed out as she retrieved the starters from the kitchen. 'Hungry?'

Vito reached for her instead of a chair. 'Only for you.'

Her bright blue eyes danced with merriment. 'Now, where did you get that old chestnut from?'

In answer Vito bent his tousled dark head and kissed her and it was like an arrow of fire shooting through her body to the heart of her. She quivered, taken aback all over again by the explosive effect he had on her. His sensual mouth played with hers and tiny ripples of arousal coursed through her. Her breasts swelled, their buds tightening while heat and dampness gathered between her legs. It took enormous willpower but she made herself step back from him, almost careening into the table in her haste to break their connection. Suddenly feeling out of control with him seemed dangerous and it *was* dangerous, she told herself, if it made her act out of character. And whether she liked it or not, everything she had done with Vito was out of character for her.

'We should eat before the food gets cold,' she said prosaically.

'I'll open a bottle of wine.'

'This is an incredibly well-equipped house,' Holly

remarked as he poured the wine he had fetched from the temperature-controlled cabinet in the kitchen.

'The owner enjoys his comforts.'

'And he's your friend?'

'We went to school together.' A breathtaking smile of amused recollection curled Vito's mouth. 'He was a rebel and although he often got me into trouble he also taught me how to enjoy myself.'

'Pixie's like that. We're very close.' Holly lifted the plates and set out the main course.

'You're a good cook,' Vito commented.

'My foster mother, Sylvia, was a great teacher. Cooking relaxes me.'

'I eat out a lot. It saves time.'

'There's more to life than saving time. Life is there to be savoured,' Holly told him.

'I savour it at high speed.'

The meal was finished and Holly was clearing up when Vito stood up. 'I feel like some fresh air,' he told her. 'I'm going out for a walk.'

From the window, Holly watched him trudge down the lane in the snow. There was an odd tightness in her chest and a lump in her constricted throat. Vito had just rebelled against their enforced togetherness to embrace his own company. He hadn't invited her to join him on his walk, but why should he have? Out of politeness? They weren't a couple in the traditional sense and he didn't have to include her in everything. They were two people who had shared a bed for the night, two *very* different people. Maybe she talked too much, maybe he was tired of her company and looking forward to the prospect of some silence. It was not a confidence-boosting train of thought.

Vito ploughed up the steep gradient, his breath steaming on the icy air. He had needed a break, had been relieved when Holly hadn't asked if she could accompany him. A loner long accustomed to his own company, he had felt the walls closing in while he'd sat surrounded by all that cosy Christmas spirit.

And that really wasn't Holly's fault, Vito conceded wryly. Even her cheerful optimism could not combat the many years of bad Christmas memories that Vito harboured. Sadly the stresses and strains of the festive season were more likely to expose the cracks in an unhappy marriage. His mother's resolute enthusiasm had never contrived to melt his father's boredom and animosity at being forced into spending time with his family.

They had never been a family, Vito acknowledged heavily, not in the truest sense of the word. His father had never loved him, had never taken the smallest interest in him. In fact, if he was honest with himself, his father sincerely disliked him. From an early age Vito had been treated like the enemy, twinned in his father's mind with the autocratic father-in-law he fiercely resented.

'He's like a bloody calculator!' Ciccio had condemned with distaste when his five-year-old son's brilliance at maths was remarked on. 'He'll be as efficient as a cash machine—just like his grandfather.'

Only days earlier, Vito's relationship with his father had sunk to an all-time low when Ciccio had questioned his son's visit to the hospital where he was recovering from his heart attack. 'Are you here to crow over my downfall?' his father had asked nastily while his mother had tried to intervene. 'My sins have deservedly caught up with me? Is that what you think?'

And Vito had finally recognised that there was no relationship left to rescue with his father. Ciccio bitterly resented his son's freedom from all financial constraints yet the older man's wild extravagance and greed had forced Vito's grandfather to keep his son-in-law on a tight leash. There was nothing Vito could do to change those hard facts. Even worse, after his grandfather had died it had become Vito's duty to protect his mother's fortune from Ciccio's demands, scarcely a reality likely to improve a father and son relationship.

For the first time Vito wondered what sort of relationship he would have with his son if he ever had one. Momentarily he was chilled by the prospect because his family history offered no encouragement.

Holly had just finished clearing up the dishes when the knocker on the front door sounded loudly. She was stunned when she opened the door and found Bill, who ran the breakdown service, standing smiling on the doorstep.

'I need the keys for Clementine to get her loaded up.'

'But it's Christmas Day… I mean, I wasn't expecting—'

'I didn't want to raise your hopes last night but I knew I'd be coming up this way some time this afternoon. My uncle joins us for lunch and he owns a small-holding a few fields away. He has to get back to feed his stock, so I brought the truck when I left him at home.'

'Thank you so much,' Holly breathed, fighting her consternation with all her might while turning away to reach into the pocket of her coat where she had left the car keys. She passed the older man the keys. 'Do you need any help?'

He shook his head. 'I'll come back up for you when I'm done.'

'I'll get my stuff together.' With a weak smile and with every sensitive nerve twanging, Holly shut the door again and sped straight upstairs to gather her belongings. She dug her feet into her cowboy boots and thrust her toiletries and make-up bag back into her rucksack.

And throughout that exercise she wouldn't let herself even think that she could be foolish enough to be disappointed at being picked up and taken home. Clearly, it was time to *leave*. She had assumed that she would have one more night with Vito but fate had decreed otherwise. Possibly a quick, unexpected exit was the best way to part after such a night, she thought unhappily. There would be neither the time nor the opportunity for awkward exchanges. She closed her rucksack and checked the room one last time. Reminding herself that she still had to pack the Christmas tree, she went back down wondering anxiously if Vito would make it back before she had to leave.

She flipped open her cardboard box and stripped the tree of ornaments and lights, deftly packing it all away while refusing to think beyond the practical. She raced into the kitchen to dump the foil containers she had used to transport the meal, pausing only to lift a china jug and quickly wash it before placing it in the box. That was that then, all the evidence of her brief stopover removed, she conceded numbly.

She didn't want to go home, she didn't *want* to leave Vito, and the awareness of that stupid, hopeless sense of attachment to him crushed and panicked her. He would probably be relieved to find her gone and he would have cringed if he saw tears in her eyes. Men didn't like messy and there could be nothing more messy or embarrassing than a woman who got too involved and tried to cling after one night. *This one-night-and-walk-away stuff is what you signed up for,* Holly scolded herself angrily. There had been no promises and no mention of a future of any kind. She would leave with her head held high and no backward glances.

All the same, she thought hesitantly, if Vito wasn't coming back in time to see her leave, shouldn't she leave a note? She dug into her rucksack and tore a piece of paper out of a notebook and leant on the table. She thanked him for his hospitality and then hit a brick wall in the creative department. What else was there to say? What else *could* she reasonably say?

After much reflection she printed her mobile-phone number at the foot of the note. Why not? It wasn't as if she was asking him to phone her. She was simply giving him the opportunity to phone if he wanted to. Nothing wrong with that, was there? She left the note propped against the clock on the shelf inside the inglenook.

Holly wore a determined smile when Bill's truck backed into the drive. She had her box and her rucksack on the step beside her in a clear face-saving statement that she was eager to get going but there was still no sign of Vito. She climbed into the truck with a sense of regret but gradually reached the conclusion that possibly it was preferable to have parted from Vito without any awkward or embarrassing final conversation. This way, nobody had to pretend or say anything they didn't mean.

Vito strode into the cottage and grimaced at the silence. He strode up the stairs, calling Holly's name while wondering if she had gone for a bath. He studied the empty bathroom with a frown, noting that she had removed her possessions. Only when he went downstairs again did he notice that the Christmas decorations had disappeared along with her. The table was clear, the kitchen immaculate.

Vito was incredulous. Holly had done a runner and he had no idea how. He walked out onto the doorstep and belatedly registered that the old car no longer lay at the foot of the lane in the ditch. So much for his observation powers! He had been so deep in his thoughts that he hadn't even noticed that the car had gone. Holly had walked out on him. Well, that hadn't happened to him before, he acknowledged grimly, his ego stung by her sudden departure. All his life women had chased after Vito, attaching strings at the smallest excuse.

But would he have wanted her to *cling*? Vito winced, driven to reluctantly admit that perhaps in the circumstances her unannounced disappearance was for the best. After all, what would he have said to her in parting? Holly had distracted him from more important issues and disrupted his self-control. Now he had his own space back and the chance to get his head clear. And that was exactly what he should want...

'When you're finished throwing up you can do the test,' Pixie said drily from the bathroom doorway.

'I'm not doing the test,' Holly argued. 'I'm on the pill. I *can't* be pregnant—'

'You missed a couple of pills *and* you had a course of antibiotics when you had tonsillitis,' her friend and flatmate reminded her. 'You know that antibiotics can interfere with contraception—'

'Well, actually I *didn't* know.' Holly groaned as she

freshened up at the sink, frowning at her pale face and dark-circled eyes. She looked absolutely awful and she felt awful both inside and out.

'Even the pill has a failure rating. I don't know...I leave you alone for a few weeks and you go completely off the rails,' the tiny blonde lamented, studying Holly with deeply concerned eyes.

'I can't be pregnant,' Holly said again as she lifted the pregnancy testing kit and extracted the instructions.

'Well, you've missed two periods, you're throwing up like there's no tomorrow and you have sore boobs,' Pixie recounted ruefully. 'Maybe it's chickenpox or something.'

'All right, I'll do it!' Holly exclaimed in frustration. 'But there is no way, just no way on earth that I could be pregnant!'

Some minutes later she slumped down on the side of the bath. Pixie was right and she was wrong. The test showed a positive. The door opened slowly and she looked wordlessly up at her friend and burst into floods of tears.

'Remember how we used to say that the babies we had would be precious gifts?' Pixie breathed as she hugged her sobbing friend. 'Well, this baby is a gift and we *will* manage. We don't need a man to survive.'

'I can't even knit!' Holly wailed, unable to concentrate, unable to think beyond the sheer immensity of the challenges she was about to face.

'That's OK. You won't have time to knit,' her friend told her, deadpan.

Holly was remembering when she and Pixie had talked innocently about their ideal of motherhood. Both of them had been born unwanted and had suffered at the hands of neglectful mothers. They had sworn that they would love and protect their own babies no matter what.

And the vague circumstances suggested by 'no matter what' had actually happened now, Holly reflected heavily, her sense of regret at that truth all-encompassing. Her baby would not be entering the perfect world as she had dreamt. Her baby was unplanned, however, but *not* unwanted. She would love her child, fight to keep him or her safe and if she had to do it alone, and it looked as though she would, she *would* manage.

'If only Vito had phoned…' The lament escaped Holly's lips before she could bite it back and she flushed in embarrassment.

'He's long gone. In fact, the more I think about him,' Pixie mused tight-mouthed, 'the more suspicious I get about the father of your child. For all you know he could be a married man.'

'No!' Holly broke in, aghast at that suggestion.

'Well, what was Vito doing spending Christmas alone out in the middle of nowhere?' Pixie demanded. 'Maybe the wife or girlfriend threw him out and he had nowhere better to go?'

'Don't make me feel worse than I already do,' Holly pleaded. 'You're such a pessimist, Pixie. Just because he didn't want to see me again doesn't make him a bad person.'

'He got you drunk and somehow persuaded you into bed. Don't expect me to think nice things about him. He was a user.'

'I *wasn't* drunk.'

'Let's not rehash it again.' Her flatmate sighed, her piquant face thoughtful. 'Let's see if we can trace him online.'

And while Pixie did internet searches on several potential spellings of Vito's surname and came up with precisely nothing, Holly sat on the sofa hugging her still-flat stomach and fretting about the future. She had already secretly carried out all those searches weeks earlier on Vito and was too proud to admit to the fact, even to her friend.

'I can't find even a trace of a man in the right age group. The name could be a fake,' her friend opined.

'Why would he give me a fake name? That doesn't make sense.'

'Maybe he didn't want to be identified. I don't know…you tell me,' Pixie said very drily. 'Do you think that's a possibility?'

Holly reddened. Of course it was a possibility that Vito had not wanted to be identified. As to why, how could she know? The only thing she knew with certainty was that Vito had decided he didn't want to see her again. Had he felt otherwise, he would have used the phone number she had left him and called her. In the weeks of silence that had followed her departure from the cottage, she had often felt low. But that was foolish, wasn't it? Vito had clearly made the decision that he had no desire to see her again.

And why should she feel hurt by that? Yes, he had said that night with her was amazing but wasn't that par for the course? The sort of thing a man thought a woman expected him to say after sex? How could she have been naive enough to actually believe that Vito had truly believed they were something special together? And now that little bit of excitement was over. What was done was done and what was gone, like her innocence, was gone. Much as her tidy, organised life had gone along with it, she conceded unhappily, because, although she would embrace motherhood wholeheartedly, she knew it would be incredibly tough to raise a baby alone without falling into the poverty trap.

CHAPTER FIVE

Fourteen months later

HOLLY SUPPRESSED A groan as she straightened her aching back. She hated parcelling up the unsold newspapers at the end of her evening shift in the local supermarket but it also meant she would be going home soon and seeing Angelo snugly asleep in his cot.

Picturing her son's little smiling face made her heart swell inside her. There was nothing Holly wouldn't do for her baby. The minute she had laid eyes on Angelo after his premature birth she had adored him with a fierce, deep love that had shaken her to the roots.

Without Pixie's help she would have struggled to survive, but, fortunately for Holly, her friend had supported her from the start. When waitressing had become impossible, Holly had taken a course to become a registered childminder and now by day she looked after her baby and two other children at home. She also worked in the shop on a casual basis. If evening or weekend work came up and Pixie was free to babysit, Holly did a shift to earn some extra cash.

And it was right then when she was thinking about how much she was looking forward to supper and her bed that it happened: she looked down at the bundle of newspapers she was tying up and saw a photograph on the front page of a man who reminded her of Vito. She stopped dead and yanked out the paper to shake it open. It was a financial broadsheet that she would never normally have even glanced at and the picture showed a man standing behind a lectern, a man who bore a re-markable resemblance to the father of her son.

'Are you nearly done, Holly?' one of her co-workers asked from the doorway.

'Almost.' Her shoulders rigid with tension, Holly was frantically reading the italicised print below the photo-graph. Vittore Zaffari, not Sorrentino. It was a man who resembled Vito—that was all. Her shoulders dropped again but just as she was about to put the newspaper back in the pile she hesitated and then extracted that particular page. Folding it quickly, she dug it into the pocket of her overall and hurriedly finished setting out the newspapers for collection.

It was after midnight before Holly got the chance to check out Vittore Zaffari online. Holly had studied the photograph again and again. He looked like her Vito but the newsprint picture wasn't clear enough for her to be certain. But the instant she did a search on Vittore Zaffari the images came rolling in and she knew without a doubt that she had finally identified her child's father.

'*My word,*' Pixie groaned, performing her own search on her tablet. 'Now I know why he gave you a fake name and was hiding out on Dartmoor. He was involved in some drugs-and-sex orgy. Hold on while I get this document translated into English.'

'Drugs and sex?' Holly repeated sickly. '*Vito?* It can't be the same man!'

But it was. The photos proved that he was *her* Vito, not some strange lookalike character. Of course, he had never been hers even to begin with, Holly reminded herself doggedly. And it was two in the morning before the two women finished digging up unwelcome facts about Vito, the billionaire banker ditched by his fabulously beautiful blonde fiancée only days before Holly had met him.

'Of course, you don't need to concern yourself with any of that nonsense,' Pixie told her ruefully. 'All you want from him now is child support and he seems to be wealthy enough that I shouldn't think that that will be a big deal.'

Holly lay sleepless in her bed, tossing and turning and at the mercy of her emotions. Vito had lied to her by deliberately giving her a false name. He too had been on the rebound but he hadn't mentioned that either. How would he react when she told him that he was a father? And did she really want to expose her infant son to a drug-abusing, womanising father? The answer to that was a very firm no. No amount of money could make a parent who was a bad influence a good idea.

But that really wasn't for her to decide, she reasoned over breakfast while she spooned baby rice into Angelo, who had a very healthy appetite. She studied her son with his coal-black curls and sparkling brown eyes. He was a happy baby, who liked to laugh and play, and he was very affectionate. Vito had been much more reserved, slow to smile and only demonstrative in bed. Holly winced at that unwelcome recollection. Regardless, Vito had a right to know that he was a father and in the same way she had a right to his financial help. She had to stop considering their situation from the personal angle because that only muddied the waters and upset her.

Angelo was the main issue. Everything came back to her son. Set against Angelo's needs, her personal feelings had no relevance. She had to be practical for his benefit and concentrate on what *he* needed. And the truth was that financially she was really struggling to survive and her baby was having to do without all the extras that he might have enjoyed. That was wrong. Her son didn't deserve to suffer because she had made a bad choice.

On the other hand, if Vito truly was the sort of guy who got involved in sex-and-drug orgies, he wasn't at all the male she had believed him to be. How could she have been so wrong about a man? She had honestly believed that Vito was a decent guy.

Even so, he was still Angelo's father and that was important. She was very much aware of just how much she had longed to know who her own father was. There was no way she could subject Angelo to living in the same ignorance. Nor could she somehow magically estimate whether Vito would be a good or bad influence on his son. The bottom line was that Angelo had the right to know who his father was so that he did not grow up with the same uncertainty that Holly had been forced to live with.

Holly acknowledged the hurt she had felt when Vito failed to make use of her phone number and contact her. Naturally her pride had been wounded and she had been disappointed. No woman wanted to feel that forgettable, but Angelo's birth had cast a totally different light on her situation. She had to forget her resentment and hurt and move on while placing her son's needs first. That would be a tall order but she believed that she loved her son enough to do it. She had to face Vito in the flesh and tell him that he was a father.

One week later, Holly handed over her package to the receptionist on the top floor of the Zaffari Bank in London. 'It's for Mr Zaffari. I would like to see him.'

The elegant receptionist set the small parcel down on the desktop and reached for something out of view. 'Mr Zaffari's appointments are fully booked weeks in advance, Miss…er…?'

'Cleaver. I believe he will want to see me,' Holly completed quietly while she wondered if that could possibly be true. 'I'll just wait over there until he's free.'

'There's really no point in you waiting,' the receptionist declared curtly, rising from her chair as two security guards approached. 'Mr Zaffari doesn't see anyone without a prior appointment.'

Stubbornly ignoring that assurance, Holly walked over to the waiting area and sat down, tugging her stretchy skirt down over her thighs. It had taken massive organisation for Holly to make a day trip to London but she knew that if she wanted to confront Vito she had to take advantage of his current presence in the UK. Her internet snooping had revealed that he was giving a speech at some fancy banking dinner that very evening and was therefore highly likely to be at the Zaffari Bank HQ throughout the day. Pixie had taken a day off to look after Angelo, and the children Holly usually minded were with their grandparents instead.

Holly had made a very early start to her day and had been appalled by the price of the train fare. Pixie had urged her to dress up to see Vito but, beyond abandoning her usual jeans and putting on a skirt with the knee boots Pixie had given her for Christmas, Holly had made no special effort. Why? As she continually reminded herself, this wasn't a *personal* visit and she wasn't trying to impress Vito. She was here to tell him about Angelo and that was all. Her restive fingers fiddled with the zip on her boots while she watched the two security guards carrying off her parcel with the absurdly cautious air of men who feared they could be carrying a bomb. Did she look like a terrorist? Like some kind of a madwoman?

Vito was in a board meeting and when his PA entered and slid a small package in front of him, which had already been unwrapped, he frowned in incomprehension, but when he pulled back the paper and saw the Santa hat and the small sprig of holly, he simply froze and gave his PA a shaken nod of immediate acceptance. Interrupting the proceedings to voice his apologies, he stood up, his cool dark eyes veiled.

What the hell was Holly doing here at the bank? Why now? And how had she tracked him down?

Hearing about that night, Apollo had scoffed. *With all your options you settled for a stranger? Are you crazy? You're one of the most eligible bachelors in the world and you picked up some random woman? A* waitress? he had scoffed in a tone of posh disbelief.

In fact, Apollo's comments had annoyed Vito so much that he had fiercely regretted confiding in his friend. He had told himself that it was for the best that Holly had walked away without fanfare, freeing them both from the threat of an awkward parting. He had also reminded himself that attempting to repeat a highly enjoyable experience invariably led to disappointment.

With the information he had had he could have traced her but he had resisted the urge with every atom of discipline he possessed. Self-control was hugely important to Vito and Holly had obliterated his self-control. He remembered that he had acted oddly with her and that memory made him uncomfortable. Even so he still hadn't forgotten her. In fact he was eager to see her because his memories of her had lingered to the extent that he had become disturbingly indifferent to other women and more particular than ever in his choices. He *wanted* to see Holly in full daylight, shorn of the schmaltzy sparkle of the festive season. He was suddenly convinced that such a disillusionment would miraculously knock him back to normality.

But why the hell would Holly be seeking him out now so long after the event? And in person rather than more tactfully by phone? And how had she linked him to the Zaffari Bank? Black brows lowering over cold dark eyes suddenly glittering with suspicion, Vito strode back into his office to await his visitor without an appointment.

Holly smiled and stood up when the receptionist approached her. In spite of her apprehension, Vito *had* remembered her and she was relieved. The Santa hat had been designed to jog his memory. After all, a male who indulged in sex parties might well not recall one night with an ordinary woman from over a year earlier. When it came to a question of morals he was a total scumbag, Holly reminded herself doggedly while walking down the corridor after another woman—even more thin and elegant—had asked her to follow her. She wondered why the other people working there seemed to be peering out of their offices in her direction and staring.

Suddenly she wondered what she was doing. Did she really want a man of Vito's dissolute proclivities in her life and Angelo's? Common sense warned her not to make snap judgements and to give Vito a chance for Angelo's sake. Her son would want to know who his dad was. Hadn't she wondered all her life who had fathered her? Hadn't that made her insecure? Made her feel less of a person than others because she didn't know that most basic fact about herself? No, Angelo deserved access to the truth of his parentage right from the start and that was what Holly would ensure her son had, no matter how unpleasant seeing Vito again proved to be.

Vito was a total scumbag, Holly reminded herself afresh while wondering why she was experiencing the strangest sense of...*elation*. Why was her heart pounding and her adrenaline buzzing? Her guide opened a door and stood back for her to enter. My goodness, he had a big office, *typical scumbag office*, she rephrased mentally. She would not be impressed; she *refused* to be impressed. And then Vito strode in through a side door and she was paralysed to the carpet because he simply looked so drop-dead amazing that she could not believe that she had ever slept with him and that he was the father of her child.

Her mouth ran dry. She felt dizzy. Butterflies danced in her tummy as she focused on those lean, darkly handsome features, and she knew that Pixie would have kicked her hard. *Total scumbag*, she told herself, but her brain would not engage with that fact and was much more interested in opening a back catalogue on Vito's sheer perfection. *To look at—perfect to look at*, she rephrased doggedly, striving to get back to the scumbag awareness. *Drugs...sex with hookers*, she fired at herself in desperation.

'The hat and the holly were an original calling card,' Vito drawled, the dark, deep accent tautening every muscle in her already tense body. 'But I *did* remember your name. I didn't need the prompt.'

Holly turned the red-hot colour of a tomato because she hadn't expected him to grasp the reasoning behind her introduction that easily.

'It would have been much easier to phone me,' Vito assured her silkily.

'And how could I have done that without your phone number?' Holly asked stiffly, because she was determined to make no reference to the fact that she had left her phone number with him and that he had decided not to make use of it. Discussing that would be far, far too humiliating.

'Well, maybe you shouldn't have run out on me before I got back to the cottage that day.' Vito smiled suddenly, brilliantly. It almost stopped her heart dead in its tracks as she stared at him. But it had not sat well with Vito that a night he had considered exceptional should have meant so much less to her that she'd walked out without a backward glance. Her reappearance satisfied him. He now felt free to study her with acute appreciation. She was wearing the most ordinary garments: a sweater, a shortish skirt, a jacket and boots, all black and all unremarkable but the glorious hourglass curves he cherished could not be concealed. His dark eyes flamed gold over the swell of her breasts below the wool and the lush curve of her hips before flying up to her full pink mouth, little snub nose and huge blue eyes. Shorn of the schmaltz and the sparkle and in full daylight, Holly was passing the test he had expected her to fail and for the first time in Vito's life, failure actually tasted sweet. He shifted almost imperceptibly as the hot swell of an erection assailed him and he almost smiled at that as well because his diminished libido had seriously bothered him.

'How did you find out who I was?' Vito enquired.

'Yes, that's right…you *lied*. You gave me a false name,' Holly was prompted to recall as she struggled to fight free of the spell he cast over her just by being in the same room.

'It wasn't a false name. I didn't lie. I was christened Vittore Sorrentino Zaffari,' he told her, smooth as glass. 'Sorrentino was my father's surname.'

That smoothness set Holly's teeth on edge. 'You lied,' she said again. 'You deliberately misled me. What I don't understand is why you did that.'

'You must appreciate that I am very well known in the business world. I prefer to be discreet. You coming here today in such a manner…' Vito shifted fluid brown fingers in an expressive dismissive gesture. 'That *was* indiscreet.' From his inside pocket he withdrew a business card and presented it to her. 'My phone number.'

Holly put the card into her jacket pocket because she didn't know what else to do with it. Indiscreet? Coming to see him in the flesh was indiscreet?

Dark golden eyes fringed by inky black, unfairly long lashes surveyed her and her tummy flipped, her heart rate increasing. 'Holly…I have the feeling that you don't understand where I'm going with this but I must be frank. I like to keep my private life *private*. I certainly do not want it to intrude when I'm at the bank. My working hours are sacrosanct.'

My word, he was literally telling her off for approaching him at his place of work, for coming to see him where other people would see her and notice her. A sense of deep humiliation pierced Holly because it had taken so much courage for her to come and confront him with the news she had. His case was not helped by the reality that she had seen a photo of him and his ex-fiancée, Marzia, posing outside the Zaffari Bank in Florence. Evidently, Marzia had enjoyed such privileges because she was someone he was *proud* to be seen with in public. Holly just could not get over Vito's nerve in daring to talk to her like that. Did he really think she was the sort of woman who would let a man talk down to her?

Her blue eyes widened and raked over him but it was pointless to try and put him down that way because she couldn't see a single flaw in his appearance. His dark grey suit fitted him like a tailored glove, outlining his height, breadth and long, powerful legs. And looking at him inevitably sent shards of mortifying memory flying through her already blitzed brain. She knew what he looked like out of his suit, she knew what he *felt* like, she also knew how he looked and sounded when he… *No, don't go there*, she urged herself and plunged straight into punitive speech because he had to be punished for putting such inappropriate thoughts into her head.

'I can't believe you're talking down to me as if you're a superior being,' Holly bit out tightly. 'Why? Because you've got money and a big fancy office? Certainly not because you've been shopped for taking drugs and sleeping with hookers!'

There was a flash of bemused surprise in Vito's brilliant dark eyes before he responded. 'That was a case of misidentification. I was not the man involved.'

'Of course you're going to say that,' Holly retorted with a roll of her eyes. 'Of course you're going to deny it to me but, as I understand it, you never once denied it in public.'

'I had a good reason for that. I never respond to tabloid journalists and I was protecting my family,' Vito returned levelly. 'I assure you…on my honour…that I was not the man involved and that I profoundly disapprove of such activities.'

Holly remained unimpressed. How did she credit that he had honour? How was she supposed to believe him? He had been protecting his family by remaining silent? How did that work?

'I do believe it would be wiser to take this meeting out of my big fancy office to somewhere more comfortable,' Vito continued, his smooth diction acidic in tone. 'I have an apartment in London. My driver will take you and you can relax there until I can join you for lunch.'

Knocked right off balance by that suggestion coming at her out of nowhere, Holly actually found herself thinking about the offer of lunch. Telling him about Angelo in an office setting felt wrong to her as well, and then a little voice in the back of her brain that sounded alarmingly like Pixie told her to wise up and think about the invitation he had made. And at that point the coin finally dropped for Holly and she grasped how Vito had chosen to interpret her sudden reappearance in his life. She wanted to kick herself for not foreseeing that likelihood, but she wanted to kick him even harder for daring to think that he could have a chance with her again. Certainly not with what she now knew about his partying habits!

'I haven't come here for another hook-up,' Holly stated with an embarrassed force that made her voice rise slightly. Behind her mortification lurked a great well of burning resentment.

Did he really think that she was so desperate for sex that she would travel all the way to London for it? How dared he assume that she was that keen, that easy? Well, she certainly hadn't taught him that she was a big challenge the night they first met, Holly conceded grudgingly. *But, my goodness, that one night must have been as good on his terms as he had said it was if he was willing to do it again.* Or maybe he was simply a sex addict? Anything was possible. When Holly had snapped back at him about his money and his fancy office and his debauched partying, she had also picked up on his surprise. He had assumed she was a quiet, easy-going little mouse but Holly wasn't quiet when her temper was roused. And right now her temper was rising like lava in a volcano. The past fourteen months had been very challenging, and working all day after a sleepless night had become her new norm. Having no way of contacting her son's father, who had handicapped her by giving her a false name, had only added to her stress.

Vito tensed. 'I didn't say anything about that. No expectations…' he murmured silkily, lean brown hands sketching an eloquent arc in the air as if to nullify her suspicions.

'Of course you have expectations…but, in this case, I'm afraid it's not going to happen. You had your chance and you blew it!' Holly snapped back, striving to hang on to her temper.

His brows drew together. 'What's that supposed to mean?'

Holly rolled her eyes, her lush mouth compressed. 'A timely little reminder that if you had really *wanted* to see me again I did leave you my phone number.'

'No, you didn't,' Vito insisted.

Holly tensed even more, angry that she had let that reminder fall from her mouth. 'I left a note thanking you for your hospitality and I printed my phone number at the bottom of it.'

Vito groaned. 'I didn't find a note when you left. Where did you leave it?'

'On the shelf in the fireplace.' Holly shrugged dismissively, keen to drop the subject.

'If there was a note, I didn't see it,' Vito assured her.

But then he would say that, wouldn't he? Holly thought, unimpressed. Of course he had found the silly note she had left behind and he had done nothing with it. And in doing nothing he had taught her all she needed to know about how he saw her. She had gone over the events of that morning in her mind many, many times. She was convinced that Vito had gone out for a walk to get a break from her. For him the fun of togetherness had already worn thin. He had ignored her note most probably because he'd been relieved to find her already gone. He had seen that night as a casual one-night stand that he had no desire to repeat.

'Whatever. It's pointless to discuss it after the amount of time that has passed. But let me spell out one fact,' Holly urged thinly. 'I *didn't* come to see you today for anything…er…physical. I came to see you about something much *more* important.'

At her emphasis, Vito raised a level dark brow in cool query mode, his wide sensual mouth tightening with impatience. And she could feel the whole atmosphere turning steadily colder and less welcoming. Naturally. She had taken sex off the lunch table, as it were, and he was no longer interested in anything she might have to say to him. And why would he be interested? She was poor and he was rich. He was educated and she was more of a self-educated person, which meant that she had alarming gaps in her knowledge. He was hugely successful and a high achiever while she worked in dead-end jobs without a career ladder for advancement. It was incredible, she finally conceded, that they had ever got involved in the first place.

'More important?' Vito prompted, his irritation barely hidden.

Defiance and umbrage combined inside Holly. She had held on to her temper but it was a close-run battle. His assumption that she was approaching him for another sexual encounter had shocked her, possibly because she had persuaded herself that they had shared something more than sex. Now she saw her illusions for the pitiful lies that they were, lies she had told herself to bolster her sagging self-esteem while she was waddling round with a massive tummy.

'Yes, much more important,' she confirmed, lifting her chin and simply spilling out her announcement. 'I got pregnant that night we were together.'

Vito froze as if she had threatened to fling a grenade at him. He turned noticeably pale, his strong bone structure suddenly clearly etched below his skin by raw tension. 'You said you were on the pill—'

Holly wasn't in the mood to go into the intricacies of missed pills and antibiotic treatment. 'You must know that every form of contraception has a failure rate and I'm afraid there was a failure. I got pregnant but I had no way of contacting you, particularly not when you had given me a fake name.'

Vito was in shock. Indeed Vito could never recall being plunged into such a state of shock before. Everything he had assumed had been turned upside down and inside out with those simple words...*I got pregnant.*

'And do you usually reintroduce yourself with a very evocative Santa hat and a sprig of holly when this happens?' he heard himself snap without even mentally forming the words. 'Is this some sort of a scam?'

Holly's small shoulders pushed up, along with her chin. 'No, Angelo is not a scam, Vito. He was born eight months after that night.'

'You come here without a word of warning and throw this announcement at me like a challenge,' Vito ground out in condemnation, no fan of major surprises in his life, as yet not even capable of thinking of what she was telling him. The prospect of having a child had long struck him as a possibility as remote as the moon. He had known fatherhood was on the cards somewhere down the line if he married Marzia but he had also known that neither of them were in any hurry to start a family.

'No, I did not. If I challenged you it would be an awful lot tougher!' Holly shot back at him furiously. 'Tough was waitressing until I was eight months pregnant and being in labour for two days before I got a

C-section. Tough is working as a childminder and a shelf-stacker and never getting enough sleep. You wouldn't know tough if it leapt on you and bit you...because in your whole blasted spoilt-rotten life you have had *everything* handed to you on a plate!'

A dark line of colour had delineated Vito's high cheekbones as he viewed her in growing disbelief. 'That is enough.'

'No, it's not enough, and you do *not* tell me when enough is enough!' Holly fired back at him, while pointing at him with an angry finger.

'Ranting at me is not getting us anywhere.'

'I'm entitled to rant if I want to rant!' Holly launched back at him an octave higher, shaking with rage and the distress she was fighting off while wondering if Vito ever lost his temper, because he was still so very controlled. 'And I don't *want* to get anywhere with you. I'm done here. I've told you that you're a father and that's why I came to see you. I saw your photo in a newspaper, incidentally...a *lovely* way to identify the father of your child! But if you want to think Angelo's a scam, you're welcome.'

'Holly...'

Holly yanked open the door and marched down the corridor very fast because she could not wait to get out of the building. She could feel the tears building up and she didn't want them to fall in front of an audience. She ignored Vito's voice when he repeated her name and stabbed the lift button with frantic force.

'Holly...*come back here*!' Vito shouted without warning.

So taken aback was she by that sudden rise in volume from him that she spun round and looked at him. He was only halfway down the corridor, evidently having expected her to return at his urging, and if looks could kill she would have been lying dead at his feet. He did have a temper, though, she registered belatedly, and it made his dark eyes glitter like gold ingots and gave his lean, darkly beautiful features a hard, forbidding edge.

Horribly aware of the number of people openly staring, Holly turned back to the lift just as the doors opened. She dived in as fast as she could but not fast enough to prevent Vito from joining her.

'You should've come back to my office.'

In silence, Holly contemplated his polished shoes because the tears were even closer now and stinging her eyes like angry wasps.

'I have to look into this situation. I need your phone number and your address,' Vito breathed in a raw undertone.

'I wasn't expecting you to be so offensive—funny, how you get the wrong idea about people. I really didn't want to get pregnant, Vito, but I love my son and he is never ever going to hear me admit that because now that he's here he's the *best* thing that ever happened to me,' she bit out shakily, hurriedly stepping out of the lift.

'Phone number. Address,' Vito said again, closing a hand to a slight shoulder to prevent her from walking away through the crowded concourse.

With a heavy sigh, Holly dug into her bag and produced a notebook. He handed her a gold pen. She squinted down at the pen, dimly wondering if it was real gold, and then scolded herself for that stupid thought. She printed out the requested details and ripped out the sheet to hand it back to him. 'Look,' she muttered uncomfortably. 'There's no pressure on you here. If I'm honest I don't really want you in our lives. You're not the sort of man I want around my son.'

And having deprived Vito of breath and speech with that damning final indictment of his character, Holly disappeared into the crowds.

CHAPTER SIX

WELL, YOU MADE a real screw-up of that, Vito reflected
for the first time in his life. But Holly hadn't given him
the smallest preparation for what was to come, so it was
scarcely surprising that everything that could go wrong
had gone wrong. He didn't react well to surprises and
the delivery of the Santa hat and the holly had seemed
suggestively sexual. Was it any wonder he had got the
wrong idea? His hard mouth compressed while he wondered about that note she had mentioned. Had she left
a note? He had looked in all the obvious places. There
had been nothing on the table or the door, and what did
it matter now anyway?

What really mattered was that without the smallest
warning he was apparently a father...

That was a mind-blowing concept but Vito was
primarily ruled by his very shrewd brain and his first
call was to his lawyer, who within the hour put him into
contact with a London-based specialist in family law.
Once all his questions had been answered, Vito was
frowning at the realisation that he didn't really have
any rights over his own son. Only marriage granted
such legal rights. He didn't consult Apollo because he
knew that his friend would start talking about demand-

ing DNA tests but he and Apollo lived very different lives and Vito was confident that if Holly had given birth to a baby eight months after that night, it could only be his baby.

He didn't know how he felt about becoming a father, and after he had organised travel to Holly's home town for the following day and informed her by text of his planned visit, he phoned his mother to break the news.

Concetta Zaffari's delight at learning that she was a grandmother tumbled through her every word and then there were questions about Holly that Vito found hard to answer, and some he skipped altogether.

'*Obviously* you'll be getting married,' Concetta trilled cheerfully, and Vito laughed that his mother should even feel the need to say that. Of course they would be getting married. No Zaffari in history had had an illegitimate child and Vito had every intention of being a better parent than his own father had proved to be, although how to go about achieving that ambition he had no very clear idea.

Holly did not respond to Vito's text because it annoyed her. Why did he assume that she was free to drop everything to make herself and Angelo available at a time that suited him? She was working an early morning shift the next day because it was a Saturday and Pixie was taking care of Angelo for her.

As a result, when Vito arrived in his limousine, having been picked up from the helicopter ride that had brought him from London, he was taken aback to be met by Pixie and informed that his son was having a nap.

'Where's Holly?' he demanded, frowning down at

the diminutive blonde, whose facial expression tele-graphed her antagonism towards him.

'At work.'

'Where?'

'The supermarket fifty yards down the road,' Pixie advanced reluctantly. 'You can wait in your car. Her shift ends in an hour.'

Infuriated that Holly hadn't thought to warn him so that he could adjust his arrival time accordingly, Vito strode down the road. He was full of righteous indigna-tion until he walked through the busy shop and caught a glimpse of Holly wheeling a trolley bigger than she was through the aisles and pausing to restock shelves. *Tough is working as a shelf-stacker and never getting enough sleep.* Abruptly, he spun on his heel and strode back out of the busy shop again, shamed by the reality that the mother of his child was being forced to work so hard to survive.

Vito would have argued that he had not been spoilt rotten, but he had been born rich and with a near-genius-level IQ, and phenomenal success in almost every field was a reward he took for granted. He had never had to struggle, never had to make the best of two bad choices, never had to do anything he didn't want to do and the sheer undeniable luxury of those realities about his life was finally sinking in on him. With uncharacteristic patience he directed his driver to take him away from the street of tiny terraced houses where Holly lived to a hotel, where he had lunch while imagining Holly going without food, which didn't im-prove his appetite.

'Vito came, then?' Holly exclaimed as she wriggled out of her overall.

Pixie nodded confirmation. 'Cheese toastie for lunch?'

'Lovely. I should've texted him to say that time didn't suit me. I don't know what it is about Vito but he makes me act completely out of character!' Holly declared guiltily.

'Take it from me, anything other than awe and flattery is probably good for Vito's character. At least he's interested in meeting his son,' Pixie said cheerfully. 'That's good news.'

Holly scoffed down the cheese toastie and touched up her make-up. She couldn't sit down, and she couldn't concentrate either. She wanted to stand at the window waiting for Vito like a kid watching out for Santa Claus arriving. Embarrassment gripped her then and she sat down, only to fly up again when Angelo cried as he wakened from his nap. Changing her son, she gave him a hug and he drank down some water to quench his thirst. It was cold in the small sitting room and she lit the fire to warm it up.

'I'm off out now,' Pixie told her while Holly was strapping a wriggling Angelo into his infant seat.

'But—'

'This is about you and him and Angelo and it's private. Give me a text when he's gone,' Pixie suggested.

Only minutes later the bell went and Holly's heartbeat leapt into her throat, convulsing it. She raced to the front door and then paused to compose herself for several seconds before opening it.

'Holly...' Vito pronounced softly, staring broodingly down at her from his great height. Sheathed in jeans and a sweater teamed with a buttery soft brown leather jacket, he totally took her breath away.

'Come in…' Her wary glance was ensnared by black-fringed dark golden eyes that sent her heart racing. 'Don't stare,' she scolded breathlessly.

'I find you very attractive. Naturally, I'm going to stare, *bellezza mia*.'

He hadn't found her attractive enough to use her phone number, Holly reminded herself ruefully. 'No, don't say insincere stuff like that. All we really have to do here is be polite to each other,' Holly told him in the small, confined hall as he came to a halt beside her.

'I can manage much more than polite,' Vito declared, his long brown fingers settling down onto her slight shoulders and feeling the rigid tension that now gripped her small frame. She had the most luscious mouth he had ever seen on a woman, pink and soft and succulent. His jeans tightened at his groin, his physical reaction instantaneous.

At his touch, Holly turned rigid with discomfiture. 'I meant friendly rather than—'

'*Maledizione!* You want me to be friendly when I can hardly keep my hands off you?' Vito shot at her with raw incredulity. 'I don't think I can manage that.'

'But you have to. I wouldn't be comfortable with anything else,' Holly told him earnestly, convinced that only disaster would follow if she allowed any further intimacy to complicate an already tense relationship.

'*Have* to?' Vito queried, a flash of glittering challenge entering his searching gaze as he stared down at her. 'Have you got someone else in your life…another man?'

Holly dealt him a startled glance. 'No… Why are you asking that?'

Without warning, Vito moved forward, pinning her up against the wall behind her. 'Because if there was

I'd probably want to kill him!' he muttered in a raw undertone.

In wonderment, Holly looked up into his lean, darkly beautiful face and then her view blurred as he hauled her up to his level and opened her mouth with the crushing demand of his own. He tasted so good, all minty and fresh, and the strength in the arms holding her felt even better. Every hard, angular line of his long, lean physique was pressed against her as he braced her hips against the wall. The passion of that hungry kiss threatened to consume her and the anomaly between the cool face he showed the world and the uncontrolled hotness hidden beneath electrified her. The piercing ache she had almost forgotten tugged cruelly in her pelvis as his tongue tangled with hers. His mouth was sublime, the feel of his unyielding muscles, hard against her softer curves, incredible. Insane chemistry…insane behaviour, she translated, pulling back from him with shell-shocked abruptness because she knew with shamed horror that all she really wanted to do with him at that moment was drag him upstairs to her bed to rediscover the amazing pleasure he could give her.

'No, this is not what you're here for…' she muttered in curt reminder, her spine stiff as she turned her back on him to walk into the small sitting room. 'You're here to meet Angelo and that's all.'

'You make it sound so simple when it's anything but simple,' Vito countered with a roughened edge to his voice because she had pushed him away and he had had to resist a powerful urge to turn caveman and yank her back to him.

'If we both make the effort, we can keep this simple and polite,' Holly stated with rigorous resolve.

'I have something I need to explain to you first...'
But by that point, Vito could see over the top of Holly's
head and his attention zeroed in so quickly on the child
in the infant seat that his voice literally trailed away.

And for Vito it was as though the rest of the world
vanished. He focused in amazement on the baby who
bore a remarkable resemblance to a framed photograph
Vito's mother had of her son at a similar age. Huge
brown eyes from below a mop of black curls inspected
him with sparkling curiosity. A chubby fist waved in the
air and suddenly Vito froze, out of his comfort zone and
hating it. He had never gone weak at the knees for pup-
pies or babies, had put that lack of a softer side down to
his grandfather's rigid discipline. But now he was looking at his son and seeing a baby with his own features in
miniature and he finally realised that the very thought
of fatherhood unnerved him. His own father had been
a hopeless parent. How much worse would he do with
Angelo when he had no idea even where to start?

Holly paused beside the child seat to say awkwardly,
'So...er...obviously this is Angelo. He's a little bored at
weekends because during the week I look after a pair
of toddlers and it's a lot livelier here.'

Vito tried to stand a little less stiffly but in truth he
felt much as if someone had swung open the door of a
lion's cage and left him to take his chances. 'Why did
you call him Angelo?'

'Because you're Italian,' Holly pointed out, wondering why he was questioning the obvious. 'I looked up
Italian names.'

Vito forced himself closer to the baby. His hands
weren't quite steady as he undid the belt strapping An-

gelo into his seat. As Vito lifted the baby, Angelo gave his father an anxious, startled appraisal.

'You're used to children,' Holly assumed, rather taken aback by that deceptively confident first move.

'No. I don't think I've ever been this close to a child before. There are none in the family and most of my friends are still single as well,' Vito told her abstractedly, wondering what he was supposed to do with the little boy now that he was holding him.

'Thank you for having him,' Vito breathed in a driven undertone. 'You could have made a different decision but you didn't.'

Nothing about this first meeting was going in any direction that Holly had foreseen. And she was even less ready to hear her baby's father thank her for not opting for a termination. Her eyes prickled with sudden emotion.

'I wanted him from the first, never had any doubts there,' she admitted gruffly. 'He's the only family I have...apart from my friend Pixie.'

As Angelo squirmed and wriggled, Vito lifted him higher and swung him round in aeroplane mode.

The baby's eyes grew huge and he let out a frightened howl before breaking down into red-faced, gulping sobs.

'Let me take him,' Holly urged in dismay as Vito lowered the squalling baby. 'He's not used to the rough stuff. There are no men in his life, really, just Pixie and me...'

Vito settled Angelo back into Holly's arms with more than a suggestion of haste and relief. 'Sorry, I upset him.'

'He needs time to get used to you,' Holly explained. 'I'll put him on the floor to play with his toys.'

Vito was tempted to back off entirely but that struck him as cowardly and he held his ground to crouch down on the rug. Finally recalling that he had brought a gift, he removed it from his pocket and tipped it out of a box. 'It's only a little toy.'

Holly winced as she noted a piece of the toy break off and fall. It had detachable tiny parts and was totally unsuitable for a baby. 'You can't give that to him,' she told Vito apologetically. 'He puts everything in his mouth and he could choke on those tiny pieces.'

In haste, Vito removed the toy and its parts again and grimaced. 'I didn't think. I really don't know anything about babies.'

Holly pulled over Angelo's toy box and extracted a red plastic truck that was a favourite. 'He likes this... Coffee?' she asked.

'Black, no sugar,' Vito murmured flatly, recognising that getting to know his son and learning how to play with him appeared to be even more challenging than he had feared.

Holly made coffee, acknowledging that she was simply delighted that Vito had had enough interest to come and meet Angelo. She could see how awkward he felt with their child and knew that if she didn't make Vito feel more comfortable he might not want to make another visit. Not that he had prepared very well for this first visit, she thought ruefully, wondering what he had thought a baby would do with a miniature brick action figure festooned in even tinier weapons.

When she returned with the coffee, Angelo was sucking on his little red truck and refusing to share the toy with his father. Holly got down on her knees beside them and, with his mother on hand, her son relaxed his grip on the truck and handed it to Vito. For an instant he looked as though he had no idea what to do with the toy and then some childhood memory of his own must have prompted him because he ran the toy across the rug making *vroom-vroom* noises and Angelo gave a little-boy shout of appreciation.

A little of Vito's tension ebbed in receipt of that favourable response. It shook him to appreciate that he had actually craved that first welcoming smile from his son. He wanted the little boy to recognise him as his father, he wanted him to like him and love him, but it was intimidating to appreciate that he hadn't the faintest idea how to go about achieving those things.

Holly parted her lips to say, 'When you first came in you said there was something that you needed to explain to me...?'

Vito's lean, strong profile clenched and he sprang upright. 'Yes. That sex-party scandal that made headlines,' he framed with palpable distaste. 'That wasn't me, it was my father, Ciccio.'

As she too stood up, Holly's mouth dropped open in shock. 'Your...*father*?'

'I didn't deny my involvement because I was trying to protect my mother from the humiliation of having her husband's habits exposed so publicly,' Vito explained grimly.

Holly dropped down on the edge of the sofa behind her. 'Oh, my goodness.'

'My mother could confirm the truth if you require further proof that I wasn't involved. What did happen that night was that I received a phone call in the early hours of the morning telling me that my father had fallen ill and needed urgent medical attention,' Vito told her, his delivery curt.

'The person calling refused to identify herself, and that should've been my warning. My mother was in Paris and I had to take charge. I wondered why my father had taken ill at an apartment owned by the bank but the minute I walked into it I could see what I was dealing with, and that I had been contacted like a clean-up crew in the hope of keeping the wild party under the radar.'

Holly nodded slowly, not really knowing what to say.

'My father had had a heart attack in the company of hookers and drugs,' Vito volunteered grimly. 'I had him collected by a private ambulance from the rear entrance and, having instructed a trusted aide to dispose of all evidence of the party, I intended to join my father at a clinic. Unfortunately the press were waiting outside when I left and I was mobbed. One of the hookers then sold her story, choosing to name me rather than my father even though I had never met her in my life. She probably lied because there was more of a story in my downfall than in that of a middle-aged married man with a taste for sleaze.'

'So you took the blame for your parents' sake?' Holly whispered in wonderment.

'My *mother's* sake,' Vito emphasised drily. 'But my mother worked out the truth for herself and she is currently divorcing my father. She looked after him until he had regained his health and then told him that she wanted a separation.'

'And how do you feel about that? I mean, their divorce means that your sacrifice was in vain.'

'I'm relieved that they've split up. I don't like my

father very much…well, not at all, really,' Vito admitted, his wide sensual mouth twisting. 'He's a greedy, dishonest man and my mother will have a better life without him.'

Utterly amazed by that flood of unrestrained candour from a male as reserved as Vito, Holly continued to scrutinise him with inquisitive blue eyes. 'Why are you telling me all this now?'

'You're family now in all but name,' Vito told her wryly. 'And I couldn't possibly allow you to continue to believe that I am not a fit person to be around my son.'

Holly fully understood that motivation and muttered, 'I'm sorry I misjudged you. I was naive to believe everything I read on the internet about you. I told you before that I don't know who my father is,' Holly admitted, wrinkling her nose. 'My mother gave me several different stories and I challenged her when I was sixteen to tell me the truth but she still wouldn't answer me. I honestly don't think she knows either. In those days she was fairly promiscuous. I've had no contact with her since then.'

'You've never had a father…much like me. Ciccio took no interest in me when I was a child and when I was an adult he only approached me if he wanted something,' he revealed, settling down with striking grace of movement into an armchair. 'My grandfather was my father figure but he was seventy when I was born and he had a Victorian outlook on childcare and education. It was far from ideal.'

Holly was fascinated by what she was learning about Vito's background, although she really wasn't sure why he was choosing to tell her so much. 'I think very few people have an ideal childhood,' she said ruefully.

'But wouldn't it be wonderful to give Angelo that ideal?' Vito pressed, black velvet lashes lifting on glittering gold as he studied her.

Her heart raced and her mouth ran dry. Hurriedly she dropped her gaze from his, only for her attention to fall to the tight inner seam of his jeans stretched along a powerful muscular thigh. Guilty heat surged through her and she shifted uneasily. 'And how could we give Angelo an ideal childhood?' she asked abstractedly.

'By getting married and giving our son a conventional start in life,' Vito spelt out with measured assurance. 'I'm not only here to meet Angelo, Holly...I'm here to ask you to be my wife.'

Disbelief roared through Holly. She blinked rapidly, doubting the evidence of her ears. He was proposing? He was actually proposing marriage to her because she had had his child?

Holly loosed an uneasy laugh and Vito frowned, because that was hardly the response he had envisaged. 'I think your grandfather's Victorian outlook is showing, Vito. We don't need to get married to give Angelo a decent upbringing.'

'How else can I be a proper father when I live in a different country?' Vito demanded with harsh bite. 'I really don't want to be only an occasional visitor in my son's life or the home he visits for a few weeks in summer when he's off school. That is not enough for me.'

Holly watched Vito lean down to lift Angelo, who was tugging at his shoelaces. He closed his arms tentatively round Angelo's small restive body and settled him down on a lean thigh. There was something incredibly sexy about his newly learned assurance with their son and her cheeks coloured at that seemingly tasteless reflection, but the smouldering edge of Vito's sexuality seemed to be assailing her every thought. 'Well, I can see that it would be difficult for you and far from ideal, but marriage...well, that's a whole different ball game,' she told him regretfully. 'I want to marry a man who loves me, not a man who accidentally got me pregnant and wants to do what he feels is the right thing by me.'

'I can't change how we conceived Angelo but with a little vision you should be able to see that where we started isn't where we have to end up,' Vito responded smoothly. 'I may not love you but I'm insanely attracted to you. I'm also ready to settle down.'

'Yes, you were engaged, weren't you?' Holly slotted in rather unkindly.

'That's not relevant here,' Vito informed her drily. 'Stay focused on what really matters.'

'Angelo,' Holly replied, with hot cheeks, while her brain trooped off in wild, unproductive circles.

He was asking her to marry him... He was actually asking her to marry him! How was she supposed to react to that when she had been astonished by his proposal?

'You should also consider the reality that eventually Angelo will be very rich, and growing up outside *my* world isn't the best preparation for that day,' Vito pointed out. 'I want to be his father. A father who is there for him when he needs me. A benefit neither you nor I enjoyed.'

He was making very valid points but Holly felt harassed and intimidated rather than grateful for his honesty. 'But marriage?' she reasoned. 'That's such a huge decision.'

'And a decision only you can make. But there would be other benefits for you,' Vito told her quietly. 'You could set up as an interior designer and live your dream with me.'

'You're starting to sound like a trained negotiator,' Holly cut in.

'I am a trained negotiator,' Vito conceded. 'But I want to give our son the very best start in life he can have, with a genuine family.'

And that was the real moment that Holly veered from consternation and fell deep into his honeytrap. Those emotive words, 'a genuine family', spoke to her on the deepest possible level and filled her head with happy images. That was a goal that she, and surprisingly Vito in spite of his privileged background, both shared, and that touched her. As she studied her son sitting peacefully in his father's arms her heart melted. She had felt ashamed of the lack of caution that had led to her pregnancy. She had been mortified that she had failed her own life goals and could not give her son the family security and the opportunities he deserved. But if she married Vito she would be able to put all her regrets behind her and *give* Angelo two parents and a stable home with every advantage.

'Even people in love find it hard to make marriage work,' Holly reminded him, fighting to resist the tempting images flooding her imagination, and to be sensible and cautious.

'We're not in love. Our odds of success may well be better because we have less exalted expectations,' Vito contended silkily. 'And our arrangement need not be viewed as a permanent trap either. In a few years, should one or both of us be unhappy, we can divorce.

All I'm asking you to do at this moment in time, Holly...
is give marriage a chance.'

He made it sound so reasonable, so very reasonable.
He was inviting her to *try* being married to him and
see if they could make it work. It was a very realistic
approach, guaranteed to make her feel that by trying
she would have nothing to lose. And she looked back
at him in silence with her heart hammering while he
raked an impatient hand through his cropped black hair.

'I'll think it over.' Holly fibbed, because she had already thought it over and really there was no contest
between what Vito was offering Angelo and what she
could hope to offer her son as a lone parent.

'Be more decisive, *bellezza mia*,' Vito urged. 'If you
marry me I will do everything within my power to
make you happy.'

Holly had known true happiness only a few times
in her life. One of those moments had been waking at
dawn enfolded in Vito's arms. Another had been the
first time she had seen her infant son. But just being
with Vito also made her happy and that worried her,
implying as it did that she was craving something more
than a very practical marriage based on their son's
needs. Should she listen to that voice of reason and
warning now? Stay on the sidelines where it was safe
rather than risk dipping her toes into the much more
complex demands of a marriage?

But at the baseline of her responses there was no
denying that she wanted Vito Zaffari with a bone-deep,
almost frighteningly strong yearning. How could she
possibly walk away from that? How could she stand
back and watch him take up with other women, as he
would, and know that she had given him that freedom?

And the answer was that she couldn't face that, would sooner take a risk on a marriage that might not work than surrender any hope of a deeper relationship with him.

Holly breathed in slow and deep and lifted her head high. 'All right. We'll get married…and see how it goes…'

And Vito smiled, that heart-stopping smile that always froze her in her tracks, and nothing he said after that point registered with her because she was washed away by sheer excitement and hope for the future.

Vito registered the stars in her eyes with satisfaction. Having been driven by the need to secure the best possible arrangement for his son's benefit, he had expended little thought on the actual reality of becoming a married man or a father. He wanted Holly and he wanted his son: that was all that mattered. And Holly would soon learn to fit into his world, he thought airily.

CHAPTER SEVEN

'SMILE!' PIXIE TOLD HOLLY. 'You look totally stupendous!'

Holly smiled to order and gripped her hands together tightly on her lap. The past four weeks had passed in a whirlwind of unfamiliar activity and changes. Now it was her wedding day and hopefully she would finally have time to draw a breath and start to relax. Only not when it was a wedding about to be attended by a lot of rich, important people, she reasoned nervously.

'How are you feeling?' she asked her best friend and bridesmaid, ruefully surveying Pixie's legs, which were both encased in plaster casts.

Her housemate had returned from a visit to her brother badly battered and bruised from a fall down the stairs, which had also broken both her legs. The extent of her injuries had appalled Holly and, although the bruising had faded, she couldn't help feeling that there was more amiss with her friend than she was letting on because Pixie's usual chirpiness and zest for life seemed to have faded away as well. And although she had gently questioned Pixie on several occasions, she could not work out if it was her own imagination in overdrive or if indeed there *was* some secret concern that Pixie wasn't yet willing to share with her.

Predictably, Pixie rolled her eyes. 'I keep on telling you I'm fine. I'll get these casts off in a couple of weeks and I'll get back to work and it'll be as if this never happened.'

'Hopefully you'll be able to come out to visit us in Italy in a few weeks' time.'

'That's doubtful.'

'Er…if it's money—'

'No, I'm not taking money off you!' Pixie told her fiercely. 'You may be marrying Mr Rich but that's not going to change anything between us.'

'All right.' Holly subsided to scrutinise the opulent diamond engagement ring on her finger. Vito wasn't the least bit romantic, she conceded ruefully, because he had sent the ring to her by special delivery rather than presenting her with it. That had been such a disappointment to her. It would have meant so much to Holly if Vito had made the effort to personally give her the ring.

'Let's simply be a normal couple from here on in,' Vito had urged, and seemingly the ring signified that normality he wanted even if it had not entailed him changing his ways.

She had wanted to ask if it was the same ring Marzia, his previous fiancée, had worn but had sealed her lips shut in case that question was tactless. And staging a potentially difficult conversation with a male she had barely seen since she had agreed to marry him had struck her as unwise.

'Of course I'm very busy now. How else could I take time off for the wedding?' Vito had enquired piously on the phone when she'd tried to tactfully suggest that he make more effort to spend some time with her and Angelo.

Vito hadn't even been able to make time for Angelo, whom he had only seen once since their agreement. Of course, to be fair, he *had* suggested that they move into his London apartment *before* the wedding and she had been ready to agree until she had heard from Pixie's brother and had realised that there was no way she could leave her injured friend to cope alone in a house with stairs. She had had to put Pixie first but Vito had not understood that. In fact Vito had called it a silly excuse that was dividing him from his son. After the wedding she needed to explain to Vito just how much of a debt she owed Pixie for her friend's support during her pregnancy and after Angelo's birth, and she needed to explain that she loved Pixie as much as she would have loved a sister. Although, never having had a sibling of his own, he might not even understand that.

And there were an awful lot of things that Vito didn't understand, Holly reflected ruefully. He had been thoroughly irritated when she'd insisted on continuing her childminding until her charges' parents had had time to make other arrangements for their care, but Holly would not have dreamt of letting anyone down, and took her responsibilities just as seriously as he took his own.

Furthermore, in every other way Vito had contrived to take over Holly and her son's lives. He had made decisions on their behalf that he had neglected to discuss with Holly. Maybe he thought she was too stupid and ignorant to make the right decisions, she thought unhappily.

First he had landed her with an Italian nanny, who had had to board at a hotel nearby because there were only two bedrooms in the house Pixie and Holly rented. London-born Lorenza was a darling and wonderful with Angelo, and Holly had needed outside help to cope with shopping for a wedding dress and such things, but she still would have preferred to play an active role in the hiring of a carer for her son.

Secondly, he had landed Holly with a horrible, pretentious fashion stylist who had wanted Holly to choose the biggest, splashiest and most expensive wedding gown ever made. Only sheer stubbornness had ensured that Holly actually got to wear her own choice of dress on her special day. And it was a very plain dress because Holly was convinced that she was too small and curvy to risk wearing anything more elaborate. She stroked the delicate edge of a lace sleeve with satisfaction. At least she had got her dream dress even if she hadn't got any input into any other details because Vito had placed all the organisation into the hands of a wedding planner, whom he had instructed *not* to consult his future wife.

In truth, Vito was extremely bossy and almost painfully insensitive sometimes. He had left it to his social secretary to tell Holly that she had a day at a grooming parlour booked for a makeover. Holly had been mortified, wondering whether Vito thought her ordinary ungroomed self was a mess and not up to his standards. Pixie had told her not to be so prickly and had asked her if she thought there was something immoral about manicures and waxing. And no, of course she didn't think that, it was just that she had wanted Vito to want her as she was, not be left feeling that only a very polished version of her could now be deemed acceptable. After all, she didn't have the security of knowing her bridegroom loved her, flaws and all, and that made a big difference to a woman's confidence, she reasoned worriedly.

'Will you stop it? And don't ask me what you're to stop!' Pixie said bluntly. 'You're worrying yourself sick about marrying Vito and it's crazy. You love him—'

'I don't love him,' Holly contradicted instantly. 'I like him. I'm very attracted to him.'

'You look him up online just to drool over his photos. If it's not love, it's a monster crush. So you might as well be married to him,' Pixie contended. 'Vito's all you think about. In fact watching you scares the hell out of me. I don't think I could bear to love anyone the way you love him, but with a little luck in time he may well return your feelings.'

'Do you think so?'

'I don't see why not,' Pixie responded thoughtfully. 'Vito's the caring type even if he hasn't yet learned to share. Why shouldn't he fall in love with you?'

But it wasn't love she felt, Holly told herself urgently. It was liking, attraction, respect, nothing more, nothing less. Loving Vito without being loved back would simply make her unhappy and she refused to be unhappy. No, she was a very hands-on person and she was going to make the most of what she *did* have with Vito and Angelo, not make the mistake of pining for what she couldn't have. After all, she could plainly see Vito in all his very good-looking and sophisticated glory and she knew she was only getting to marry him because some crazy fate had deposited her as a damsel in distress on his doorstep one Christmas Eve night.

Her foster mother, Sylvia, pushed Pixie down the aisle in her wheelchair while Holly walked to the altar, striving not to be intimidated by the sheer size of the church and the overwhelming number of unfamiliar faces crammed into it. Vito stood beside a guy with black shoulder-length hair and startling green eyes whom she recognised from online photographs as his best friend, Apollo Metraxis. Holly only looked at the bronzed Greek long enough to establish that he was giving her a distinctly cold appraisal before her attention switched quite naturally to Vito, who, unromantic or otherwise, was at least managing to smile that breathtaking smile of his.

Her heart bounced around in her chest to leave her breathless and when he closed his hand over hers at the altar she was conscious only of him and the officiating priest. She listened with quiet satisfaction to the words of the wedding ceremony, grinned when Angelo let out a little baby shout from his place on Lorenza's lap in a front pew and stared down all of a glow at the wedding band Vito threaded smoothly onto her finger. It was her wedding day and she was determined to enjoy it.

When they signed the register, she was introduced to a smiling older woman clad in a lilac suit and hat with diamonds sparkling at her throat.

'I'm Vito's *mamma*, Concetta,' the attractive brunette told her warmly. 'I've met my grandson. He *is* beautiful.'

Unsurprisingly, Holly was charmed by such fond appreciation of her son and her anxiety about how Vito's mother might feel about his sudden marriage dwindled accordingly. Concetta, it seemed, was willing to give her a fighting chance at acceptance. Vito's friend Apollo, however, could barely hide his hostility towards her and she wondered at it. Didn't he realise that this marriage was what Vito had wanted? Did he think she had somehow forced his friend into proposing? Holly's chin came up and her big blue eyes fired with resolution because she was happy to have become Vito's wife and Angelo's mother and she had no intention of pretending otherwise.

After some photos taken at the church they moved on to the hotel where the reception was being held. 'There are so many guests,' she commented with nervous jerkiness when they climbed out of the limo, an easier exercise than it might have been because Holly's closely fitted gown did not have a train.

'My family has a lot of friends but some guests are business acquaintances,' Vito admitted. 'You shouldn't be apprehensive. Invariably wedding guests are well-wishers.'

Apollo's name was on her lips but she compressed it. She didn't think much of the Greek for deciding he disliked her, sight unseen. What happened to giving a person a fair chance? But she refused to allow Apollo's brooding presence to cast a shadow over her day. And although Apollo was supposed to be Vito's best man, and Pixie the chief and only bridesmaid, Apollo snubbed Pixie as well. Of course, he had brought a partner with him, a fabulously beautiful blonde underwear model with legs that could rival a giraffe's and little desire to melt into the background.

As was becoming popular, the speeches were staged before the meal was served. Holly's foster mother, Sylvia, had insisted on saying a few words and they were kind, warming words that Holly very much appreciated. Concetta Zaffari had chosen not to speak and Vito's father had not been invited to the wedding. When Apollo stood up, Holly stiffened and the most excruciating ex-

perience of her life commenced with his speech. In a
very amusing way Apollo began to tell the tale of the
billionaire banker trapped by the snow and the waitress
who had broken down at the foot of the lane. Holly felt
humiliated, knowing that everyone who had seen Angelo and worked out her son's age was now aware that
he had been conceived from a one-night stand.

Vito gripped her hand so hard it almost hurt and
hissed in her ear, 'I did not know he was planning to
tell our story!'

Holly said nothing. She wasn't capable of saying anything, meeting Pixie's compassionate gaze across the
circular table, recognising Concetta Zaffari's compas-
sion on her behalf in her gentle appraisal. She could
feel her face getting hotter and hotter and pictured herself resembling a giant blushing tomato and it was a
mercy when Apollo had concluded his maliciously polite speech, which had left her pierced by a dozen poi-
sonous darts of condemnation. He had outed her as a
slut at the very least and a gold-digger at worst because
he had made it sound the most impossible coincidence
that her car had gone off the road at that convenient
point. But worst of all, he had not uttered a single lie.

'What a bastard!' Pixie said roundly when she had
contrived to follow Holly into the palatial cloakroom.
'Vito's furious! He asked me to come and see that you
were all right.'

'I shouldn't be ashamed of being a waitress or a
woman who fell pregnant after a one-night stand,' Holly
muttered apologetically. 'But somehow sitting there in
front of all those richly dressed, bejewelled people I
felt like rubbish.'

Sylvia joined them at that point and put her arms

around Holly. 'That young man's a rather nasty piece of work,' she opined ruefully. 'That was a very inappropriate speech, in the circumstances. Holly…sticks and stones may break your bones but words can never hurt you.'

'Not true.' Holly sighed, breathing in deep. 'But don't worry about me. I can handle it—'

'But you shouldn't have to on your wedding day, as I told your bridegroom,' Pixie framed angrily.

'No, no, let it go,' Holly urged ruefully. 'I've got over it already. I was being oversensitive.'

Her foster mother departed and Pixie said several rather unrepeatable things about Apollo Metraxis before the two women began to make their way back to the function room. And then suddenly Pixie stopped her wheelchair and shot out a hand to yank at Holly's wrist to urge her into the alcove in the corridor. She held a finger to her lips in the universal silencing motion and Holly frowned, wondering what on earth her friend was playing at.

And then she heard it, Apollo's unforgettable posh British accent honed by years of public schooling. 'No, as you know, he wouldn't listen to me. *No* DNA test, *no* pre-nup…get this? He *trusts* her. No, he's not an idiot. It's my bet he's playing a deeper game with this sham marriage. Maybe planning to go for full custody of his son once he has them in Italy. Vito's no fool. He simply plays his cards close to his chest.'

Holly turned deathly pale because there was not the smallest doubt that Apollo was talking about her and Angelo and Vito. For a split second she honestly wished she hadn't eavesdropped and she could see by her friend's expression that Pixie was now regretting the impulse as well because of what they had overheard. But without a word she planted firm hands on the handles of the wheelchair and moved her friend out of the alcove and back towards the function room.

But Holly was shattered inside and her expressive face was wooden and, after one glance at her, Vito whirled her onto the dance floor and closed his arms round her. Rage with Apollo was still simmering inside Vito like a cauldron. Well aware of his friend's attitude towards his marriage, Vito blamed himself for still including him in the event. He had naively assumed that, after meeting Holly, Apollo would realise how outrageous his cynical outlook was when it came to her. But his misplaced trust in the Greek billionaire had resulted in his bride's hurt on what he very well knew she believed should be a happy day. Even worse, he was still recovering from the unprecedented surge of raw protective reaction he had experienced during that speech. Any individual who wounded Holly should be his enemy, certainly not a trusted confidant of many years' standing.

'I'm sorry, really sorry about Apollo's speech,' he told her in a driven undertone. 'If I'd had the slightest idea what he was planning to say—'

'You should've kept your mouth shut about how we met,' Holly told him in an unforgiving tone. 'If you hadn't opened your big mouth, he wouldn't have known—'

'Holly…I didn't know that we were going to end up together—'

'No, that came right out of left field with Angelo, didn't it?' Holly agreed in a saccharine-sweet tone he had never heard from her before. 'Just boy talk, was it? The brunette slapper I pulled at Christmas?'

Dark colour rimming his high cheekbones, Vito gazed down at her with dark eyes blazing like golden flames. 'Are you seriously saying that you didn't tell Pixie about us?'

Hoist by her own petard, Holly reddened and compressed her lips.

'Thought so,' Vito said with satisfaction and she wanted to slap him very hard indeed. 'We both spoke out of turn but you have the kinder and wiser friend.'

'Yes,' Holly conceded gruffly, tears suddenly shining in her eyes.

'I have spoken to Apollo. If it's any consolation I wanted to punch him for the first time in our long friendship. He's a hothead with a very low opinion of marriage in general. His father married six times,' Vito explained ruefully. 'I know that doesn't take away the sting but, speaking for myself, I don't care how many people know how I met my very lovely, very sexy wife and acquired an even cuter baby. You're a Zaffari now. A Zaffari always holds his or her head high.'

'Is that so?' Holly's heavy heart was steadily lightening because it meant a lot that he was perceptive enough to understand how she felt and that he had made his friend aware that he was angry about that speech.

'Yes, *gioia mia.* We Zaffaris take ourselves very seriously and if one is lucky enough to find a waitress like you in the snow he's grateful for it, not suspicious. Apollo and I have a friendship based very much on the fact that we are opposites in character. He distrusts every woman he meets. He's always looking for a hidden agenda. It must be exhausting,' he said wryly.

Holly rested her brow against his shoulder as they slow-danced and she let the mortification and the anger seep slowly out of her again. It was being with Vito that was important, being with Vito and Angelo and becoming a family that really mattered. And in her heart of hearts she could not credit that Vito was planning a sham marriage purely to try and deprive her of their son. That accusation was hopefully the suggestion of a troubled, misogynistic mind, she reasoned hopefully.

'This is *your* jet...like really? *Your own jet?*' Holly carolled incredulously a few hours later when she scanned the ultra-opulent leather interior of the private jet.

'I travel a great deal. It's convenient,' Vito parried, amused by her wide, shaken eyes.

'As long as sleeping with the cabin crew isn't included,' Holly whispered, her attention resting on the more than usually attractive team overseeing the boarding of Lorenza and Angelo and all the baby equipment that accompanied her son. In consternation Holly realised that she had accidentally spoken that thought out loud.

Predominantly, Vito was shocked by the concept of having sex with anyone who worked for him and then he looked at his bride's burning face and he started to laugh with rare enjoyment. 'No, that sort of entertainment is probably more Apollo than me. Although I did take advantage of *you.*'

'No, you didn't,' she told him before she hurried forward to grasp her son, having missed him during her enforced break from him throughout the day.

'Older, wiser, plied an innocent with wine...' Vito traded, condemning himself for his crime for her ears alone. 'But if I had the chance to go back I would *still* do it again.'

Encountering a lingering sidewise glance from black-fringed dark golden eyes, Holly felt heat lick through her pelvis as she took a seat and cuddled Angelo. For possibly the first time since she had conceived she looked back at that night in the cottage without guilt and regret. No, on that score Vito had hit a bullseye. Given the chance, in spite of the moments of heartache and stress along the way, she would also still have done the same thing again.

And if Vito could be that honest, why shouldn't she match him? Tell him about the phone call she had overheard Apollo making? She would pick her moment, she decided ruefully, and she would ask if he had ever thought of their marriage as a sham and if she had anything to worry about.

Angelo was asleep by the time they landed in Italy. Holly had freshened up, noting with disappointment that her outfit hadn't travelled very well. The fashion stylist had tried to persuade her to buy a whole host of clothes but with Vito already paying for the wedding and her gown she hadn't felt right about allowing him to pay for anything else before they were married. She had teamed an elegant navy-and-white skirt with a matching top but her get-up had creased horribly and looked as though she had worn it for a week rather than only a few hours. Straightening it as best she could, she wondered if Vito would even notice.

Holly was enchanted by the wonderful scenery that enfolded as the four-wheel drive moved deeper into the countryside. Charming low hills rolled across a landscape peacefully dotted with cypresses, serrated lines of fresh green vines and silvery olive groves. Medieval villages slumbered on hilltops while ancient bell towers soared into the cloudless blue sky. Occasionally she caught a glimpse of beautiful, weathered old farmhouses nestling among the greenery and the wild flowers and she wondered if Vito's home resembled them.

'There it is…the Castello Zaffari,' Vito announced with pride as the car began to climb a steep ribbon of road. Dead ahead Holly glimpsed a building so vast it covered the whole hilltop like a village while elaborate gardens decorated the slopes below it. She froze, convinced that that could not possibly be his home because it was a palace, not a mere dwelling. A giant domed portico denoted the front entrance where the car came to a halt.

'Is this it? Is this where you live?' Holly asked in a small voice, wondering crazily if she could hide in the car and refuse to emerge until he admitted that the palace wasn't really his and he had only been joking. It *had* to be a joke, she thought fearfully, because no ordinary woman could possibly learn to live in the midst of such medieval splendour.

Vito picked up on the edge in her voice and frowned at her. 'Yes. What's wrong?'

'Nothing,' she said hurriedly as she took Angelo to allow the nanny to climb out.

'Don't you like it?'

'Of course I like it,' Holly lied in a rush, utterly overpowered by the huge building as she accompanied Vito into a massive marble-floored hall studded with matching lines of columns. 'But you could've at least hinted that you lived like royalty.'

'I don't,' Vito incised in firm rebuttal. 'I live in a historic building that has belonged to my family for centuries. I live a very average, normal life here…'

Please tell me he didn't say that, Holly argued with herself as they rounded the gigantic centrepiece of a winding stone staircase and were faced with a long assembled row of what could only have been household staff all dressed up in uniform as though they had strayed off the set for *Downton Abbey. Average? Normal?* On what planet was Vito living?

Sick with the nervous unease of someone totally out of their comfort zone, Holly fixed a smile to her stiff face while Vito conducted introductions. There was a great deal of billing and cooing over Angelo and Vito's own former nanny, Serafina, surged forward to take the baby. Apart from her, Silvestro was the head honcho in the household and little giggly Natalia, it turned out, was Holly's English-speaking maid. With great difficulty Holly kept her face straight at the prospect of having a maid and watched while the two nannies carried Angelo off upstairs.

'Natalia will show you to our room,' Vito informed her at the foot of the stairs and then he paused, a frown etching between his level brows, his dark eyes semi-concealed by his ridiculous lashes as he murmured, 'I should have asked you—do you object to sharing a room?'

The planet he was on was definitely far, far from the moon, Holly thought crazily as she raised her brows. 'Where else would I sleep?'

'Obviously you could have your own room,' Vito told her valiantly.

And Holly almost burst out laughing because Vito was being his extraordinarily polite self and going against his own instincts. She could see it in the tension etched in his lean, darkly handsome face, hear it in the edge roughening his dark, deep drawl. He really, *really* didn't want her to choose a separate bedroom and she wondered why on earth he had made the offer. 'No...' Holly reached for his clenched hand. 'You're not getting rid of me that easily,' she teased.

Vito laughed and smiled almost simultaneously and all the tension vanished. *Silly, silly man*, she thought warmly as she followed Natalia up the stairs. Why had he even given her a choice? Separate bedrooms? Was that how husband and wife normally lived in such a gigantic house? How his parents and grandparents had lived? Well, from here on in Vito was going to have to learn how a normal, average couple lived, and having shared a bed with him once had only made her all the keener to repeat the experience, she acknowledged, her colour rising. But there was just no way of denying that the most unbearable hunger clenched her deep down inside when she looked at Vito.

Months had passed since that night in the cottage but she had learned a lot about herself after that first educational experience. Other men hadn't tempted her the way Vito had and she had always assumed that that'd meant she wasn't a very sensual person. Vito, however, had unleashed her newly discovered appetite for intimacy and taught her differently. He was definitely the right man for her. She could only hope that she would prove to be the right woman for him.

Natalia opened the doors of what had to be the most drop-dead ugly bedroom Holly had ever seen. It was truly hideous. Heavy dark drapes shut out most of the light and made the vast room gloomy. A material that looked and felt like dark red leather covered the walls and every other surface from the high, elaborately moulded and domed ceiling to the furniture, which was heavily gilded in gold. Holly swallowed hard. It looked as though it hadn't been decorated in at least a hundred years and it was very possible that the weird paper was antique like the furniture.

Well, Holly thought as her maid cast open the doors to show her around what appeared to be an entire suite of rooms for their use, she might be keen to share a bedroom with Vito but he might have to move the location of the shared bedroom to make her happy. Natalia beamed and showed her into a large room walled with closets, which she swept open to display the contents.

'Who does all this belong to?' Holly asked, recoiling while wondering if all the garment-bag-enclosed items of clothing had been left behind by Vito's former fiancée, Marzia.

'Is *your* gift…is *new*,' the brunette stressed while showing off a still-attached label to what appeared to be a hand-embroidered ballgown of such over-the-top glamour that it took Holly's breath away.

A gift that could only be from Vito. The gift of an entire wardrobe of clothes? Holly fingered through drawers packed with lingerie and nightwear in little decorative bags and stared at the racks of shoes and accessories Natalia was eager for her to see and appreciate. It was a mind-blowing collection and it was just way too much altogether for Holly, after the wedding, the massive palace Vito lived in and his revealing query about whether or not she was willing to share a bedroom with him. What on earth? What on earth kind of marriage was she in that he had told her so little about his life and yet bought her so much? Did he think flashing around his money made up for his failure to explain all the other stuff?

Catching a glimpse of her creased and tousled reflection in one of the many mirrors in the dressing room, Holly almost groaned. She didn't want to get tricked out in fancy clothes, she simply wanted comfort, and as Natalia opened Holly's single case on the now seemingly pitiful assortment of clothing that had been her lot pre-Vito, Holly bent down to scoop out her one extravagance: a shimmering maxi dress with an iridescent sheen that skimmed her every curve with a flattering fit. She was relieved to see that while the bedroom belonged to a bygone age, the en-suite bathroom, while palatial, was contemporary. Stepping into a wonderful walled rain-forest shower, she rinsed away the tired stickiness of travel and tried to let her anxieties float off down the drain with the soapy water.

A marriage was what you made of it and she had no intention of underestimating the challenge ahead. They had married for Angelo's benefit but their son could only enjoy a happy home life if his parents established a good relationship. Holly's childhood had been damaged by her mother's neglect and self-indulgence, Vito's by his father's indifference. He should've warned her about the giant historic house and the extravagant new wardrobe, but she could no more shout at him for being richer and more pedigreed than she had estimated than she could shout at him for his unvarnished generosity.

Dressed, her black hair tumbling freely round her shoulders, Holly explored the connecting rooms Natalia had briefly walked her through earlier. A door stood ajar on the balcony that led off the sitting room and she strolled out, watching the sun go down over the stunning landscape and the manicured gardens below and slowly veil them in peach, gold and terracotta splendour. Sounds in the room she had vacated alerted her to the arrival of a trolley, and the rattle of cutlery fired her appetite and drew her back indoors.

Vito was framed by a doorway at the far end of the room, his suit abandoned in favour of jeans and a white shirt open at his strong brown throat. Her tummy was awash with butterflies as she instinctively drew in a deep breath and savoured her view of him. He stood there, so tall and dark and devastatingly handsome, watching her with the assessing eyes of a hawk.

Vito finally tore his gaze from his bride's opulent curves, that were so wonderfully enhanced by the fine fabric of her dress, but the words he had been about to speak had vanished from his brain. Holly, he acknowledged simply, was an incredibly sexy woman. Innate sensuality threaded her every movement. It was there in her light gliding walk, the feminine sway of her hips, the swell of her breasts as she straightened her spine and angled her head back to expose her throat.

He had expected Apollo to recognise the sheer depth of Holly's natural appeal, but he couldn't be sorry that his friend's distrust had blinded him because when Vito had seen some of his guests look at his bride with lustful intent, it had annoyed the hell out of him. And that new possessive, jealously protective streak about what was *his* disturbed Vito, who was immensely suspicious of emotional promptings. He had always chosen women who brought out the rational side of his nature but Holly incited much more primal urges.

Vito's butler, Silvestro, moved forward to pour the

wine with a flourish and light the candles on the circular table. Holly tasted the wine with an appreciative sip.

'It's an award-winning Brunello my grandfather laid down years ago. This is a special occasion,' Vito pointed out as he dropped lithely down into his seat and shook out his napkin.

'I cut my teeth on wines that tasted like vinegar.' Holly sighed. 'I'm not much of a drinker.'

'Why would you be if it tasted that bad?' Vito asked with amusement.

'Why didn't you warn me that you lived in a vast house your family have owned for centuries?' Holly asked quietly.

'It didn't occur to me,' Vito admitted with a frown.

'This place was a shock…as was the new wardrobe.'

'You were supposed to shop for clothes at the same time as you chose your wedding dress but the stylist said you weren't interested. So I took care of it for you.'

'Thank you, I suppose…'

As Silvestro left the room, having drawn the trolley close to enable them to serve themselves, Holly embarked on the tiny delicate parcels on her plate. They were exquisitely displayed, and the oriental flavours tasted phenomenal. The courses that followed were even better. Holly had never eaten such fabulous food before.

'Who does the cooking here?' she asked.

'I have a very well-paid chef on staff. When I'm staying at one of my other properties he travels ahead of me.'

Bemused by the concept of a mobile personal chef, Holly blinked. 'You have *other* properties?'

'Here I have the apartment in Florence and a villa

on the shores of Lugano in Switzerland. Those were in-
herited. But I also own property in the countries I visit
most frequently,' Vito admitted.

Holly was frowning. 'What's wrong with hotels?'

'I don't like them. I like quiet and privacy, particularly when I'm working,' Vito advanced smoothly. 'It's
my sole extravagance.'

'When I called you a spoilt-rotten rich boy I wasn't
far off the mark,' Holly dared.

'Had you ever met my grandfather you would never
have awarded me that label. He was a rigid disciplinar-
ian with a punitive approach. He thought my mother
was too soft with me.' A rueful smile brought a gentler
than usual curve to Vito's wide sensual lips. 'He was
probably right.'

'Your grandfather sounds very judgemental. I don't
think I would've liked him very much.'

'He was a dinosaur but a well-intentioned one. Since
he passed away two years ago, however, I have insti-
gated many changes.'

Holly dealt him a sidewise glance and whispered
conspiratorially, 'Our bedroom is a complete horror.'

A flashing grin illuminated Vito's lean, dark features. 'Really?'

'Very dark and depressing.'

'I think I've only been in that room once in my life.'

Her brow furrowed. 'You mean it wasn't yours?'

'No, it's simply the main bedroom in the house and
Silvestro has been trying to move me in there ever since
my grandfather departed,' Vito confided with amusement. 'But I always resist change and I need the allure
of a wife there to entice me.'

Holly compressed her lips as she sipped her wine. 'I

have no allure,' she told him, wrinkling her snub nose in embarrassment.

Vito laughed, lounging back in his chair to study her with gleaming dark golden eyes. 'Being unaware of it doesn't mean you don't have it. In fact that very lack of awareness is incredibly appealing.'

'I should check on Angelo.'

'No, not tonight, *bella mia*,' Angelo intoned as he sprang upright to reach for her hands and raise her slowly from her seat. 'Tonight is ours. Angelo has two nannies and an entire household devoted to his needs. After all, he is the first child in the Zaffari family for a generation, and as such more precious than diamonds to our staff.'

Her throat tightened as he looked down at her with glittering golden eyes fringed by ridiculously long lashes. Suddenly she couldn't breathe or move. 'Er... what are we standing here for?'

'I want to see this horror of a bedroom,' Vito said thickly and then he lowered his head and sealed his mouth to hers with hungry, driving urgency.

Like a flamethrower on a bale of hay his passion ignited hers with instantaneous effect. Her arms closed round him, her small hands roving up over his strong, muscular back to cling to his shoulders. His tongue slid moistly between her lips and an erotic thrill engulfed her in dizzy anticipation. Her nipples prickled into tingling tightness while damp heat surged between her legs. She pressed her thighs together, struggling to get a grip on herself but still wanting him so much it almost hurt...

CHAPTER EIGHT

HAULING HOLLY UP into his arms, Vito carried her into the bedroom and settled her on the foot of the bed to remove her shoes.

'I didn't appreciate how dark it was in here,' Vito admitted as he switched on the bedside lamps. 'Or how hideous. My grandfather liked grand and theatrical.' He sighed.

Holly scrambled back against the headboard and studied him with starry eyes. He stood half in shadow, half in light, and the hard, sculpted planes and hollows of his lean, strong face were beautiful. She marvelled at the fate that had brought two such different people together and rejoiced in it too. Liking, respect, attraction, she listed with resolution inside her head, buttoning down the stronger feelings battling to emerge, denying them.

'Did your parents occupy separate bedrooms?' she asked curiously.

'It was always the norm in this household. I didn't want it for us.' Vito came down on the bed beside her. 'If you only knew how much I've longed for this moment. I wanted you with me in London *before* the wedding.'

'But it couldn't be done. I had responsibilities I couldn't turn my back on.' Holly sighed.

'I could've made arrangements to free you of those duties.'

'Not when they're dependent on friendship, loyalty, and consideration for other people,' Holly disagreed gently, lifting a hand to follow the course of his jutting lower lip and note the stubborn angle of his strong jaw-line. 'You can't rearrange the world only to suit you.'

'*Sì*...yes, I can,' Vito declared without shame.

'But that's *so* selfish—'

'I will not apologise for being selfish when it comes to your needs and Angelo's.' Vito marvelled at her in-ability to appreciate that he would always place their needs over the needs of others. What was wrong with that? It was true that it took a certain amount of ruth-lessness and arrogance, but he had fought hard in life for every single achievement and saw nothing wrong with an approach that maximised the good things for his family and minimised the bad. The way he saw it, if you made enough effort happiness could be balanced as smoothly as a profit-and-loss column.

With his strong white teeth he nipped playfully at the reproving fingertip rapping his chin.

Holly startled and then giggled and sighed. 'What am I going to do with you?'

'Anything you want… I'm up for *anything*.' Vito sa-voured her, his dark golden eyes holding hers with ex-plicit need for a heartbeat. He pushed her back against the pillows and then his mouth claimed hers with hun-gry, delicious force.

Heat unfurled in her pelvis. Her heart raced and the tension went out of her only to be replaced by a new kind of tension that shimmied through her bloodstream like an aphrodisiac and made her heart race. Her breath came in quick, shallow gasps between kisses, each leading into the next until he rolled back and, having established that there was no helpful zip, he gathered the hem of her dress in his hands and tugged it up over her body and over her head to pitch it aside.

'That's better,' he growled, pausing to admire the picture she made in her pretty bridal lace lingerie.

'Except you're still wearing far too many clothes,' Holly objected, embarking on his shirt buttons.

Vito yanked off his shirt without ceremony, kicked off his shoes, peeled off his socks, only to halt there, his long, lean frame trembling while Holly's hands roamed over the hills and valleys of his hard, muscular abdomen. Her reverent fingers took a detour to follow the furrow of dark hair vanishing below the waistband of his jeans.

'I missed you,' she said truthfully. 'I missed *this*…'

Unfreezing, lean dark features rigid with control, he unsnapped his jeans and vaulted off the bed to take them off. 'It was the best night of my life, *bellezza mia.*'

And yet he still hadn't made any mention of seeing her again that night or the following morning. That still stung and Holly said nothing. Had he really not seen her note? Could she believe that?

'That note I left at the cottage for you—' she began breathlessly.

'I didn't see it.'

'Would you have phoned if you'd had my number?' she prompted in a reckless rush.

'I don't know,' Vito responded quietly. 'Certainly I would've been tempted, but on another level I distrust anything that tempts me.'

His honesty cut through her. Even if he had found the

note, he wouldn't have phoned her, she decided painfully. He would have written off their night of passion as a once-in-a-lifetime experience and left it behind. That hurt, but there was nothing she could do about it. She wanted to know who else had since shared his bed but it wasn't a question to be asked on their wedding night even though her heart cried out for reassurance. It would be an unfair question when he had not owed her loyalty. Of course there had been other women in the months they had been apart. That was yet another pain she had to bear.

'I've never wanted a woman the way I want you,' Vito told her thickly.

He flung a handful of condoms down by the bed and stripped naked without inhibition while she watched.

Pink washed Holly's face because he was fully aroused and ready.

'I couldn't get enough of you that night and that unnerved me,' he framed abruptly. 'You were a very unexpected discovery.'

He reached for her again, deftly skimming off her bra and panties, twisting his hips away when she tried to touch him. 'No... If you touch me, you'll wreck me. I'm on a hair trigger after months of abstinence,' he growled, lean brown hands roving over the full curves of her breasts, lingering over her pink pointed nipples to tug and tease until little sounds she couldn't silence broke from between her lips.

Vito flung back the sheet and settled her beneath him to pay serious attention to her swollen mouth and the glorious swell of her breasts.

'Months of abstinence?' Holly encouraged helplessly, her breath tripping in her throat as he sucked on a protruding bud while long, skilled fingers stroked her thigh.

'I'm not an easy lay,' he told her. 'I'm very, very fussy.'

'Nothing wrong with that,' Holly framed in ragged reassurance, all the feeling in her body seemingly centred between her thighs where she was scarily desperate for him to touch her.

And then he did and she gasped and her eyes closed and the fire at the heart of her grew hotter still, hips shifting up and from side to side, the drumbeat of need awakened and throbbing and thrumming through every skin cell. Vito shifted down the bed and parted her thighs. He knew exactly what he was doing. She had discovered that the night Angelo was conceived.

He teased her with the tip of his tongue, slow and then quicker until she could no longer stay silent and whimpers and gasps were wrenched from her. A long sure finger stroked through her wet folds and she quivered, every nerve ending jumping to readiness as the excitement crept higher.

At the height of her climax she cried out his name, lost in the convulsive spasms of erotic pleasure. She was so lost in that pleasure that she struggled to remember what day it was and even where she was. Her lashes flickered when she heard him tear open a condom. As he returned to her she wrapped both arms round him possessively, her body temporarily sated.

He pushed her back and drove into her with a guttural groan of satisfaction. 'Like wet satin,' he bit out appreciatively.

Hunger sizzled through her as his bold shaft stretched her and sank deep. Suddenly she was sensually awake again, her body primed as he angled his lean hips to ensure that she received the maximum enjoyment. His hunger for her was unhidden, his strokes were hard and fast, tormentingly strong. The ache low in her body pinged and climbed in intensity. She wanted, oh, *how* she wanted, craved, needed and longed for that maddening pulse of yearning to be answered, overwhelmed. And then her spine was arching and her body jerking and the waves of hot, drenching pleasure were like a shooting star flaming through her and setting her on fire with the wondrous release from her own body.

'Sexiest, most amazing woman ever...and *mine*,' Vito husked in her ear, his weight heavy on her as he rolled over and pulled her down on top of him. 'That's the most important fact. You're mine, *gioia mia*.'

'Are you mine too?' Holly whispered dizzily.

'*Sì...*'

'Is sex always this good?'

'Not even half the time. We have our own unique variety of fireworks.'

Holly rested her cheek on a damp bronzed shoulder, her body replete. He smelled so good she drank him in like a drug. She liked being his. She liked that possessive note she heard edging his dark drawl because it made her feel less like Angelo's mother and more like Vito's wife, valued, needed and wanted on her own account. Long fingers traced the path of her spine as he shifted position.

'I have an impossibly fast recovery time with you,' Vito husked, sliding her back onto the sheet on her front, lingering on the soft full curves of her behind.

He reached for another condom. Holly didn't even lift her head. She was still in that place somewhere between total satiation and awareness, shifting obediently as he eased a pillow below her hips, raising her, rear-ranging her to his satisfaction. And then she felt him rigid and full at her entrance where she was now tender and swollen. He drove in hard and she came suddenly fully awake, eyes wide, throat catching on a breath, heart hotwired back into pounding. He buried himself deep and it felt so good she moaned.

'I like the little sounds you make.' He ground into her with power and energy and a spontaneous combustion of heat surged at the apex of her body.

Excitement crowned with her every cry and snatched breath. She couldn't breathe against the onslaught of raw, surging excitement. With every savage thrust he owned her in a way she had never thought to be owned and she gave herself up to the rise of the hot, pulsing pleasure. The excitement crested with white-hot energy and the sweet waves of deep, quivering pleasure consumed her. Winded, she slumped back down into the pillows.

'Shower time,' Vito told her, lifting her out of bed. 'You're not allowed to go to sleep yet.'

'You and your son have a lot in common.'

'We're both very attached to you?' Vito urged her into the shower.

'You don't sleep at night,' she contradicted. 'Although I have to admit that you're more fun than he is in the middle of the night. Angelo gets grouchy when he's teething.'

'I won't get grouchy with you in my bed,' Vito assured her, leaning back against the tiled wall, lean, bronzed and muscular, a study in male perfection.

Holly was like an energy drink, releasing his tension, refreshing him, leaving him feeling amazingly relaxed. Vito had never done relaxed and wasn't quite sure how to handle it. It was a great deal easier simply to concentrate on working off that surplus energy in bed.

Even with the honeyed ache of sex and satiation Holly wanted to put her hands all over him and explore him with the freedom she had restrained on their first night together. She was so comfortable with him, so indescribably comfortable it almost spooked her. 'I can sleep standing up,' she warned him, resting her damp head down on a strong brown shoulder.

'I have to work tomorrow, *bellezza mia*. Make the most of *now*,' Vito murmured huskily, gathering her close.

Her eyes opened very wide on the tiled wall. He had to work the day after their wedding? Was there some crisis on?

'No. I just like to work,' Vito confided lazily, as if there were nothing the slightest bit strange about his desire to act as though the day after their wedding were just like any other day.

'Are you taking *any* time off?' It was a loaded question but she tried to make it sound casual and unconcerned and then held her breath.

'I'll be home every night...you can bet on that,' Vito growled, nipping at the sensitive flesh below her ear until she shivered helplessly against him and his big hands rose to cup and massage her breasts. 'I'll be keeping you very much occupied.'

Sex, she thought dully. Nothing wrong with his enthusiasm in that department but was that really all he was interested in, all he had ever been interested in? Or simply all she had to offer? Her teeth gritted. What did she have to offer in the intellect category? No, she was never going to be his equal there. Were they going to be one of those couples who never interacted except when their child was around? Would she chatter on relentlessly about Angelo and only ever really get Vito's attention in bed? It sounded a sad and desperate role to her but what was she going to do about it? She couldn't *make* him want more or force him to see her in a different light, could she?

A sham marriage? That overheard phone call returned to haunt her. How hard could it be for Vito to fake being genuinely married when all he intended to do was have sex with her? A chill trickled through her tummy and made her tense. Suddenly fears that she had earlier dismissed were becoming a source of genuine concern. Why had she so easily believed that Apollo was talking nonsense about Vito's intentions? Apollo Metraxis had known Vito since childhood. Apollo probably knew Vito a great deal better than she did and if he suspected that Vito had only married her to gain custody of his son, shouldn't she be sincerely scared?

When she wakened it was still dark, with only the faintest glimmer of light showing behind the curtains. She was deliciously comfortable. Vito had both arms wrapped round her and she was snuggled up to him, secure in the warmth and the wonderfully familiar scent of his skin. He was stroking her hip bone and she stretched in a helpless little movement.

'I want you, *tesoro mia*.'

Her eyes flew wide as he shifted against her back, letting her feel the hard swell of him. *'Again?'*

His sensual mouth pressed into the sensitive skin of her throat. 'Don't move. I'll do all the work.'

And he did, repositioning her, gently rousing her

from her drowsiness and then sinking into her with exquisite precision. She heard herself gasp and then moan and the sweet swell of pleasure surged up and overpowered all her anxious thoughts. Excitement took hold and she trembled with need as his smooth thrusts rocked her sensitised body. She couldn't fight her responses or the uncontrollable wave of ecstatic sensation that swept her to an explosive climax.

'What a wonderful way to wake up,' Vito groaned into her tumbled hair. 'I never dreamt that having a wife could be so much fun. Are you joining me for breakfast?'

Behind her hair, Holly rolled her eyes. She was married to one of those horrid people who came alive around dawn and acted as though it were late morning. Either she stayed in bed and saw very little of him or she changed herself to fit. She lay listening to the shower running and watched him emerge swathed in a towel, the long, lean length of his unspeakably beautiful body mostly exposed. Her mouth ran dry as he disappeared into the dressing room and opened another door. Closet doors were rammed back, drawers opened and closed. She scrambled out of bed and ran for the shower before she could be tempted to backtrack and fall back asleep. Dabbing on minimal make-up, she brushed her hair and extracted some of her new clothes to wear because a pair of jeans and a washed-out cotton top didn't seem quite sufficient for the grandeur of the Castello Zaffari.

Clad in beautifully tailored chinos and a filmy blouse in autumn shades, she slotted her feet into canvas shoes and went out to join Vito. He looked as he had the day she had confronted him at the Zaffari Bank: cool, sophisticated, remote, very much the banker. And at the same time he contrived to look amazing whether he was slotting cufflinks into his cuffs or brushing his cropped black hair.

'Who wears cufflinks these days?' Holly prompted.

Vito shrugged. 'We all use them at the bank.'

'Not at the cutting edge of fashion, then,' she mocked, although his dark suit was incredibly well tailored to lovingly shape wide shoulders, a broad chest, narrow hips and long, powerful legs. Just looking at him, she wanted to touch him.

'Breakfast,' he reminded her, heading for the door.

The *castello* was silent until they reached the ground floor where vague signs of industry could be heard somewhere in the distance. Silvestro entered the hall and looked taken aback to see them. He burst into Italian and Vito responded with quiet amusement.

'Why does everybody think I should be staying home today?' he quipped, leading the way into a sunlit dining room.

'Maybe…because you should be?' Holly dared. 'Just married and all that…'

Silvestro fussed round the table making unnecessary adjustments while Vito translated all the many options Holly could choose for breakfast. As the older man sped off Vito lifted one of the financial newspapers piled at his end of the table and began to read it and Holly wondered whether she should have stayed in bed. She wanted to go and see if Angelo was awake but she didn't want to leave Vito lest he leave for the bank while she was gone.

She had already decided to confront Vito about that phone call she had overheard Apollo making but she had intended to pick and choose the right moment, which might well have been while they were still wrapped round each other in bed. But something about the way Vito lifted that newspaper after dragging her downstairs awakened her temper.

'I overheard Apollo talking on the phone to someone at our reception yesterday.'

Vito lowered the newspaper and frowned at her. 'Overheard?' he questioned.

Below the onslaught of his dark glittering gaze, Holly went pink. 'Well, eavesdropped…I suppose.'

'Are you in the habit of listening in on other people's phone calls?'

'That's not really relevant here,' Holly fudged in desperation, feeling like a child being called to account for misbehaviour. 'Apollo was so obviously talking about us…about our marriage. He was saying that you hadn't had a DNA test with Angelo and that there had been no pre-nup—'

'You're trying to shock me with facts?'

Holly scrambled out of her seat and squared her small shoulders. 'Apollo was sneering about his belief that you trust me.'

'Obviously I won't be trusting you in the vicinity of confidential phone calls,' Vito pronounced, deadpan.

Somehow the confrontation was not proceeding in any expected direction and Holly was stung into anger. 'Apollo thinks our marriage is a sham!'

Vito elevated an ebony brow. 'I think the only two people who can comment on that probability are the two of us.'

'Apollo seemed to believe that you had only married me to get me to move to Italy. He thinks you're planning to go to court and try to claim full custody of our son.'

'I'm not sure whether to be more offended by my friend's low take on my morals or by my wife's,' Vito imparted very softly, marvelling that she could have placed credence in such an unrealistic plot, which smacked very much of Apollo's sensational outlook on life. 'Do you think I would do that to you and Angelo?'

'That's not the point,' Holly protested.

'It is exactly the point,' Vito incised with ruthless bite. 'Why else are you challenging me with this non-sense?'

As Silvestro reappeared with a tray Holly sank back down into her seat. She was angry and mortified at the same time but clung to the comforting fact that Vito had called her concerns 'nonsense'. While food was being laid on the table, Holly studied her pale pink nails and suspected that one day she might possibly throw a cof-fee pot at Vito for his sarcastic cool.

'To clarify matters,' Vito mused as Silvestro re-treated, 'Apollo was most probably talking to a mu-tual friend called Jeremy, who happens to be a lawyer trained in family law. Although it is ridiculously unnec-essary, Apollo tries to protect me from the gold-diggers of this world. If it is any consolation he was no keener on Marzia. He would never marry without a pre-nuptial agreement in place. I deemed it unnecessary because I would not marry a woman I couldn't trust. You're being naive and insecure.'

Holly bridled at that blunt speech. 'I don't see how.'

With precise movements that set her teeth on edge, Vito poured a cup of black coffee. 'I would not deprive my son of his mother. I was sent to boarding school abroad at the age of seven, Holly. I was incredibly

homesick and unhappy. Do you honestly think I would
subject Angelo to anything similar?'

Holly studied her cup of tea with wooden resolve.
Her face was so hot she could feel her ears heating up
in concert. No, she could not see him planning to do
anything that would damage their son. Boarding school
abroad at the tender age of seven? That was brutal, she
thought helplessly.

'I *love* my son. I will try hard never to hurt him and
I know how much he needs his mother,' Vito framed
with measured cool. 'I am also an honourable man. I am
not deceitful in personal relationships. I married you in
good faith. If eavesdropping on Apollo can rouse your
suspicions to this level, what are our prospects for the
future? Trust has to work both ways to be effective.'

Holly swallowed hard. Vito was annoyed with her for
doubting him and for paying heed to a stupid phone call
she shouldn't have been listening to in the first place.
She wasn't sure she could blame him for that. On the
other hand his determination to head to the bank the day
after their wedding was hardly likely to boost her confidence in his attitude towards either her or their marriage.

How much did Vito value her? Just how unimport-
ant was she in his desire for a marriage that would not
interfere in his inflexible daily schedule? To thrive, all
relationships needed compromise, commitment and the
luxury of time spent together. Didn't he appreciate that?
And if he didn't, was she clever enough to teach him
that she could offer him something more worthwhile
than sex? That was a tall order.

Vito rose from his chair and studied her in brooding silence. 'By the way, we're dining out this evening
with friends.'

Holly looked up in surprise. 'What friends?'

'Apollo and his girlfriend and Jeremy Morris and his wife. They're currently staying on Apollo's yacht with him.'

The prospect of spending an evening in Apollo Metraxis's radius appealed about as much to Holly as a public whipping. She frowned, studying Vito with incredulous eyes. 'Knowing how I feel about Apollo, why would you arrange something like that?'

Vito compressed his stubborn mouth. 'He's a close friend. He made a mistake. You need to get over it.'

Temper threw colour into Holly's cheeks. 'Do I, indeed?'

Vito gazed expectantly back at her. 'I want it all smoothed over and forgotten…'

'Right, so that's me got my orders, then.' Holly lifted her chin.

'It's not an order, Holly, it's advice. I'm not dropping a lifelong friend because you don't like him.'

'And isn't there some excuse for that dislike?'

'Apollo didn't tell any lies about how we met. Remember that,' Vito retorted with succinct bite.

A painful flush illuminated Holly's face.

'Why shouldn't we have a night out?' Vito fired at her in exasperation. 'I thought you would enjoy getting dressed up and socialising—most women do.'

'That's not my world,' Holly breathed in taut objection.

'It is *now*,' Vito pointed out without hesitation, his impatience unconcealed. 'You need to make an effort to fit in. Why do you think I bought you all those clothes? I want you to have the expensive trappings and to *enjoy* having them.'

As Vito strode out Holly held her breath, feeling a

little like someone trying to fight off a panic attack. He had voiced truths she didn't really want to face. This was his world and, in marrying him, she had become part of that world. He saw no reason why his life shouldn't continue the way it always had and he was making no allowances for Holly's insecurities. No, it was her job to swallow her ire with Apollo and be nice. Well, that certainly put her in her place, didn't it? Vito's long-standing friendship with the Greek billionaire meant more to him than his wife's loss of face at her own wedding. Just as work still meant more to him than settling into marriage and fatherhood. Vito, she recognised painfully, was highly resistant to change of any kind...

CHAPTER NINE

AFTER LUNCH THE same day, Holly lifted Angelo out of the high chair in the dining room and walked outside to settle the baby on a rug already spread across the grass. Her son beamed as she arranged several toys within his reach, enjoying the change of scene.

'Tea,' Silvestro pronounced with decision, having followed her, and he sped off again. Holly made no comment, having already learned that Silvestro liked to foresee needs and fulfil them before anyone could make a request and, truthfully, she did fancy a cup of tea.

She cuddled Angelo and studied the bird's-eye view of the gardens spread out below in an embroidered carpet of multi-hued greens with occasional splashes of colourful spring flowers. Daily life at the Castello Zaffari promised to be pretty much idyllic, she reflected ruefully, feeling ashamed of her negative thoughts earlier in the day when Vito had left her to go to work.

Here she was on a permanent holiday in a virtual palace where she ate fabulous food and was waited on hand and foot. She had beautiful clothes, an incredibly handsome, sexy husband and a very cute baby. What was she complaining about? For the first time ever since Angelo's birth she also had free time to spend with her son. As for the dinner outing? That was a minor hiccup and, having examined her new wardrobe, she had decided to follow the 'little black dress rule' rather than risk being over-or underdressed for the occasion.

A woman in a sunhat with a basket over her arm walked up a gravelled path towards her. Holly tensed, recognising her mother-in-law, Concetta Zaffari.

'Are you on your own?' the small brunette asked. 'I thought I had seen Vito's car drive past earlier but I assumed I was mistaken.'

'No, you weren't mistaken. He's at the bank,' Holly confirmed, as the older woman settled down beside her to make immediate overtures to Angelo.

'Today? My son went into work *today*?' his mother exclaimed in dismay.

Holly gave a rueful nod.

'He should be here with you,' Concetta told her, surprising her.

The rattle of china and the sound of footsteps approaching prompted Holly to scramble upright again. She handed Angelo to Concetta, who was extending her arms hopefully and chattering in Italian baby talk. The two women sat down by the wrought iron table in the shade while Silvestro poured the tea. He had magically contrived to anticipate the arrival of Vito's mother because he had brought an extra cup and a plate of tiny English biscuits.

'A honeymoon isn't negotiable. It should be a given,' Concetta pronounced without hesitation.

'If Vito wants to work, well, then he wants to work,' Holly parried, tactfully non-committal.

'You and this darling little boy are Vito's family

and you must ensure that my son puts you first,' Vito's mother countered. 'That is very important.'

Holly breathed in deep. 'Vito loves to work. I don't feel I have the right to ask him to change something so basic about himself.'

'Priorities have to change once you're married and a parent. As for having the right...' The older woman sipped her tea thoughtfully. 'I will be open with you. I saw your distress after Apollo made that unsuitable speech at the wedding yesterday.'

Holly winced. 'I was more embarrassed than distressed...I think.'

'But why should you be embarrassed by this gorgeous little boy?' Concetta demanded. 'Let me tell you something... When I married Vito's father, Ciccio, thirty-odd years ago, I was already pregnant...'

Holly's blue eyes widened in surprise at that frank admission.

Concetta compressed her lips. 'My father would never have allowed me to marry a man like Ciccio in any other circumstances. He knew that Ciccio was a fortune hunter but I was too naive to see the obvious. I was eighteen and in love for the first time. Ciccio was in his thirties.'

'That's a big age gap,' Holly remarked carefully.

'I was an heiress. Ciccio targeted me like a duck on a shooting range,' the brunette declared with a wry twist of her lips, 'and I paid a steep price for being young and silly. He was unfaithful from the outset but I closed my eyes to it because while my father was alive divorce seemed out of the question. Only when Ciccio dragged our son's reputation down into the dirt with his own did I finally see the light.'

'The scandal in the newspapers?' Holly slotted in with a frown, fascinated by the elegant brunette's candour.

'I could not forgive Ciccio for saving himself at Vito's expense.'

'Vito wanted to protect you.'

'That hurt,' Concetta confided tautly. 'It hurt me even more to see Vito falsely accused and slandered but it also let me see that he was an adult able to handle the breakdown of his parents' marriage. Now I'm making my middle-aged fresh start.'

'It's never too late,' Holly said warmly, noticing how Angelo's sparkling dark eyes matched his father's and his grandmother's.

Concetta confided that she regularly took the flowers from the garden at the *castello* as arranging them was her hobby. Holly admitted that she had never arranged a flower in her life and urged the older woman to keep on helping herself. Vito's mother promised to continue doing the flowers for the house and the two women parted on comfortable, friendly terms.

Holly spent what remained of the day doing her hair and her nails and refusing to think about the evening ahead. Thinking about it wasn't going to change anything. Apollo was Vito's friend and he thought highly of him, she reminded herself. Unfortunately it didn't ease the sting of the reality that her husband seemed to rate Apollo more highly than he rated his wife.

Vito collected her in a limo. He wore a sleek dinner jacket. 'I used my apartment to change,' he admitted, smiling as she climbed into the car. 'You look very elegant.'

But as soon as Holly arrived at the restaurant and saw the other two women she realised she had got it wrong in the frock department because she had played it too safe. Apollo's girlfriend, Jenna, wore a taupe silk dress that plunged at both back and front and was slit to the thigh, while Jeremy's wife, Celia, wore a short fitted scarlet dress that showed off her very shapely legs. Holly immediately felt frumpy and dumpy in her unexciting outfit, wishing that at the very least she had chosen to wear something that displayed a bit of cleavage.

While the men talked, Celia shot inquiries at Holly and it was no surprise to discover that the highly educated and inquisitive redhead was a criminal lawyer. Having her background and educational deficiencies winkled out and exposed made Holly feel very uncomfortable but her attempts to block Celia's questions were unsuccessful and she was forced to half turn away and chat to Jenna to escape the interrogation. Jenna, however, talked only about spa days and exclusive resorts.

'You've never been on a ski slope?' she remarked in loud disbelief.

'I'll teach Holly to ski,' Vito sliced in, smooth as glass.

Holly paled because the idea of racing down a snowy hill at breakneck speed made her feel more scared than exhilarated. As the entire conversation round the table turned to ski resorts and talk of everyone's 'best ever runs', she was excluded by her unfamiliarity with the sport. Jenna's chatter about hot yoga classes and meditation were matched by Celia's talk about the benefits of an organic, *natural* diet, ensuring that Holly felt more and more out of her depth. She was also bored stiff.

'How do you feel about yachting?' Apollo asked smoothly across the table, his green eyes hard and mocking. 'Do you get seasick?'

'I've never been on a yacht, so I wouldn't know. I'm fine on a fishing boat or a ferry, though,' she added with sudden amusement at the amount of sheer privilege inherent in such a conversational topic.

'Who took you fishing?' Vito asked her abruptly.

'Someone way before your time,' Holly murmured, unwilling to admit in such exclusive company that it had been a rowing-boat experience with a teenaged boyfriend.

'Way to go, Holly! Keep him wondering.' Celia laughed appreciatively.

Her mobile phone vibrated in her bag and she pulled it out. 'Excuse me. I have to take this,' she said apologetically, and rose from the table to walk out to the foyer.

It was Lorenza phoning to tell her that Angelo had finally settled after a restless evening. Aware that her son was teething, Holly had asked the nanny to keep her posted. On the way back to the table she called into the cloakroom. She was in a cubicle when she heard Jenna and Celia come in.

'What on earth does a guy like Vito see in a woman like her?' Jenna was demanding thinly. 'She's like a little brown sparrow beside him.'

Angry resentment hurtled through Holly and in the strangest way it set her free to be herself.

'Jeremy thinks Vito must have had a pre-nup written up by another lawyer,' Celia commented. 'There's no way Vito hasn't safeguarded himself.'

Emerging, Holly washed her hands and glanced at the aghast pair of women frozen by the sinks. 'At least I've got a wedding ring on my finger,' she pointed out to Jenna. 'You have to be at least number one hundred in Apollo's long line of companions.'

'We had no idea you were in here,' Celia began sharply, defensively.

'Ah, Celia,' Holly pronounced gently, flicking the tall redhead a calm appraisal in turn. 'I can assure you that there is no pre-nup. My husband *trusts* me.'

And with that ringing assurance, Holly turned on her heel, head held high, and walked back out to the table. And she might resemble a little brown sparrow, she thought with spirit, but she was married to a guy who found little brown sparrows the ultimate in sex appeal. Amused by the level of her own annoyance, Holly returned to her seat and in a break in the conversation addressed Apollo. 'So where's the best place for me to learn to ski?' she asked playfully.

Vito dealt her a bemused look and watched her begin to smile at Apollo's very detailed response because Apollo took his sports very seriously.

A deep sense of calm had settled over Holly. She was still furious with Vito for subjecting her to such an evening with very little warning but, having stood up for herself and spoken up in her own defence, she felt much more comfortable. After all, she could be herself anywhere and in any company. The only person able to make her feel out of her depth was herself and she was determined not to let those insecurities control her reactions again. So, she was more accustomed to stacking shelves in a shop and occasional trips to the cinema but she could do spa days and skiing and yachting trips if she wanted to. It was Vito's world but that wedding ring on her finger confirmed that now it was her world as well and she needed to remember that.

She would have to adapt. But Vito had to learn to adapt too, she reflected grimly. He had told her over the breakfast table that she had to trust him, but so far he had done little to earn that trust. And so far, Holly had been the one to make all the changes. She had given up her home, her country, her friends, and her entire life to come to Italy and make a family with Vito. True, it was a gilded life but that didn't lessen the sacrifices she had made on her son's behalf. When was Vito planning to become a family man, who put his wife and his child first?

'You've been very quiet,' Vito remarked as Holly started up the stairs.

'I want to check on Angelo.'

'There is no need.'

'There is every need. I'm his mother,' Holly declared shortly. 'It's immaterial how efficient or kind your staff are, Vito. At the end of the day they are only employees and none of them will ever love Angelo the way I do. Don't ever try to come between me and my son!'

In silence, Holly went up to the nursery, tiptoeing across the floor to gaze down at the slumbering shape of her little boy lying snug in his cot. Smiling, she left the nursery again.

'I wouldn't try to come between you,' Vito swore.

Holly ignored him and went down to their bedroom, kicking off her shoes before stalking into the bathroom.

'Holly...' Vito breathed warningly from the doorway.

'I'm not speaking to you. You have a choice,' Holly cautioned him thinly. 'Either we have silence or we have it out. *Choose.*'

Vito groaned. 'That's not much of a choice.'

'It's the only one you're going to get and probably more than you deserve.' Holly dabbed impatiently at her eyes with a cotton pad and eye-make-up remover.

'Have it out, I suppose,' Vito pronounced very drily.

Holly tilted her chin. 'You had no business forcing me out to that dinner tonight because I wasn't ready for it. I was uncomfortable, of course I was. Two days ago I was living in an ordinary world with ordinary jobs and meeting ordinary people and now I'm in this *weird* new environment,' she framed between compressed lips. 'And I know everyone seems to think I'm in clover and it *is* wonderful not to have to worry about money any more, but it's strange and it's going to take me time to get used to it. You haven't given me any time. You expect *me* to make all the changes...'

Vito had paled. 'You're making valid points. I'm not a patient man.'

'And you don't always live up to your promises either. You said you'd do everything within your power to make me happy,' Holly reminded him doggedly. 'Then you go back to work within a day of the wedding even though you have a son you barely know and a wife you don't know much better. If you want me to trust you, you have to show me that you value me and Angelo, that we're not just new possessions to be slotted into your busy life and expected not to make any waves. You have to give us your time, Vito, take us places, show us around our new home.'

Holly was challenging him and he hadn't expected that from her. She had thrown his words about trust back at him. And she was also telling him that he was already failing dismally in the successful husband stakes. He had married her one day and walked away the next, acting as though a wedding ring were more than sufficient proof of his commitment.

And had Holly been Marzia it *would* have been sufficient. Marzia had wanted that ring and his lifestyle. She would have thrown a party to show off the *castello* and she would have invited all the most important socially connected people to act as her admiring audience. She would have spent half the day at a beauty salon and the other half shopping for couture garments designed to impress. Vito had lost count of the number of times he had returned to the town house he had once shared with Marzia only to discover that they were hosting a dinner when he was longing for a quiet evening. Marzia had been easily bored and had needed others to keep her entertained. Holly, in comparison, asked for and expected very little. In fact she was asking for something she shouldn't have had to ask for, he acknowledged with a grim look in his dark, unusually thoughtful gaze.

Family came first…*always*. Even his workaholic grandfather had never put the bank before his family. What had he been thinking of when he'd left Holly and Angelo to amuse themselves? They needed him and he hadn't spared them a thought.

'And tonight?' Vito prompted.

'It was bearable. I heard Celia and Jenna bitching about me but I stood up for myself and I couldn't care less about their opinions. But I would've been more equipped to enjoy myself and relax if I'd had more time to prepare.'

'I screwed up,' Vito acknowledged broodingly.

'Yes,' Holly agreed, sliding into bed while he still hovered. 'And sometimes I'll screw up. That's life.'

'I'm not used to screwing up,' Vito told her.

'Then you'll try harder not to make the same mistakes again,' Holly riposted sleepily.

* * *

Holly slept in the following morning. She woke with a start, showered and pulled on jeans to pelt upstairs and spend some time with Angelo. In surprise she stilled in the doorway of the nursery bathroom when she saw Vito kneeling down by the side of the bath and engaged in dive-bombing plastic boats for Angelo's amusement. She had simply assumed that Vito had gone into the bank as usual but it was clear that at some stage, even though he had dressed for work, he had changed his mind. His jacket and tie were hooked on the radiator, his shirtsleeves rolled up.

'Vito…'

Raking damp, tousled black hair off his brow, Vito turned his head and flashed her a heart-stopping grin. 'Angelo emptied his cereal bowl over his head at break-fast and I decided I should stay home.'

Holly moved forward. 'I can see that…'

'I'm very set in my ways but I believe I can adapt,' he told her, laughing as Angelo smacked the water with a tiny fist and splashed both of them.

'He'll grow up so fast your head will spin. You won't ever get this time back with him.' She sighed. 'I didn't want you to miss out and then live to regret it.'

'You spoke up and that was the right thing to do. I respect your honesty. Parenting is a whole new ball game and I still have to get my head around it,' Vito confided, snatching down a towel and spreading it on the floor before lifting Angelo's squirming little body out of the bath and laying him down.

'How to get yourself soaked!' Holly groaned.

'I'm already drenched to the skin,' Vito riposted with quiet pride. 'Angelo and I have had a lot of fun.'

The nursery was empty and Holly rustled around gathering the necessities. 'What have you done with the nanny posse?' she asked curiously.

'I told them to take a few hours off. Being so new to this I didn't want an audience.'

Holly dried Angelo and deftly dressed him. Vito un-buttoned his wet shirt, the parted edges revealing a bronzed sliver of muscular torso. Together they walked downstairs.

'Do you have any photographs of when you were pregnant?' Vito asked, startling her into turning wide blue eyes onto his lean, dark face.

'I don't think so…I wasn't feeling very photogenic at the time. Why?'

'I'm sorry I missed all that. Something else I can't get back,' Vito conceded gravely. 'I really would have liked to have seen you when you were carrying our child.'

Regret assailed her, for she would have loved to have had his support during those dark days of worry and exhaustion. She had struggled to stay employed and earning for as long as possible so as not to be a bur-den on Pixie.

'As for that challenge you offered me,' Vito mused, walking back to their bedroom to change. 'Draw up a list of places you would like to go.'

'No lists. I'm phobic about lists,' she told him truth-fully. 'Let's be relaxed about what we do and where we go. No itineraries laid out in stone. Are you taking time off?'

'Of course. But I'll catch up with my email in the evenings,' he warned her. 'I can't completely switch off.'

'That's OK,' she hastened to tell him. 'But you may be bored.'

'Not a chance, *gioia mia*,' Vito riposted as he cast off his wet shirt. 'You and Angelo will keep me fully occupied from dawn to dusk and beyond.'

'And beyond' was very much in Holly's mind as she studied his muscular brown torso, a tiny burst of heat pulsing between her thighs. It was the desire she never really lost around Vito. Her colour heightened. She was so pleased, so relieved that he had listened to her, but there was a fear deep down inside her that she would not have enough to offer to satisfy him outside working hours.

'When was the last time you saw your mother?' Vito asked lazily as they lay in bed six weeks later.

Holly stretched somnolent limbs still heavy with pleasure and rolled her head round to face him, bright blue eyes troubled. 'I was sixteen. It wasn't the nicest experience.'

'I can deal with not nice,' Vito volunteered, closing an arm round her slight shoulders to draw her comfortingly close.

Holly felt gloriously relaxed and shockingly happy. With every day that passed she was increasingly convinced that Vito was the man of her dreams. He was everything she had ever wanted, everything she had ever dreamt of. But even better, he had proved that he was capable of change.

Six weeks ago, she had reminded Vito that he had to learn how to be part of a family instead of an independent operator seeing life only from a work-orientated point of view. He had started out wanting to make up lists and tick off boxes as if that were the only route to success. He had a maddening desire to know in advance exactly what he would be doing every hour of every day and had only slowly learned to take each day as it came.

Holly had spent several days creating a mood board of her ideas on how to redecorate their hideous bedroom. While she was doing that, Vito had learned how to entertain Angelo. Settling on a colour palate of soothing grey enlivened with spicy tangerine accents, Holly had ordered the required products and utilised a local company to do the actual work. Throughout the entire process, Vito had shown depressingly little curiosity, merely agreeing that it was many years since the *castello* had been decorated and that, as his mother had never had any interest in revitalising the interior, he was sure there was plenty of scope for Holly to express her talents.

Leaving the work team to handle the decorating project, Holly and Vito had taken their son to stay on the shores of Lake Lugano. Vito's family had bought a Swiss villa because, like Zurich and Geneva, Lugano was a major financial centre. Over the generations the Zaffari bankers had found the shores of the lake a convenient business location to stash the family while they worked.

At the villa they had thrown open the shutters on the magnificent lake views and enjoyed long lazy meals on the sun-dappled *loggia*. By day they had explored the water in a private boat, stopping off to ramble around the picturesque little villages on the rugged shoreline. Some evenings they had sat on the lake terrace drinking garnet-coloured Brunello di Montalcino wine while they watched the boats sailing by with twinkling lights. Other nights they had strolled round the cobbled lanes in Lugano to pick a quiet restaurant for dinner, but none had yet lived up to the perfection on a plate offered by Vito's personal chef.

They had visited the Zoo al Maglio, where Angelo had been enchanted by the antics of the monkeys and had struggled fiercely to copy them. They had caught the funicular railway to the top of Monte San Salvatore to enjoy the alpine scenery and on the way back they had stopped off at a chocolate factory, where a peckish Holly had eaten her weight in chocolate and had sworn never to eat it again while Vito teased her about how much he adored her curves.

There had been shopping trips as well, to the designer boutiques on the Via Nassa, where Holly had become bored because her new wardrobe was so expansive she saw no reason to add to it. She had much preferred the bustling liveliness of the farmers' market in the Piazza Riforma, from which she had returned home carrying armfuls of the flowers she couldn't resist. Discovering that arranging them was more of an art than a matter of simply stuffing them in a big vase, she had resolved to ask her mother-in-law for some tips.

'Your mother…' Vito reminded her. 'Are you going to sleep?'

'No. It's only two o'clock in the afternoon.' But in truth she was already smothering a yawn because their post-lunch nap had turned into a sex-fest. 'Mum…' she reminded herself. 'It was the last time I ever lived with her. I thought she wanted me back because I was no longer a child who needed looking after twenty-four-seven. I thought she finally wanted to get to know her daughter. But I got it all wrong—'

'How…?' Vito asked, long fingers inscribing a soothing pattern on her hip bone.

'Mum was living with a guy who owned a little supermarket. She asked me to help out in the shop...' Holly's voice trailed away ruefully. 'It was a crucial school year with exams and I didn't want to miss classes but she insisted she couldn't cope and I fell for it—'

'And...?' Vito prompted when she fell silent again.

'It turned out that she only wanted me working in the shop to save *her* having to do it and they weren't even paying me minimum wage. I was just cheap labour to please her boyfriend and give her a break.' Holly sighed. 'I missed so much school that social services took me back into care. Of course I failed half my exams as well. I haven't seen her since. I realised that she was never going to be the mother I wanted her to be and I had to accept that. She wasn't the maternal type—'

'And yet you're so different with Angelo.'

'And if you compare your relationship with your father, aren't you different with Angelo too? We both want to give our son what we didn't have ourselves,' Holly murmured, rejoicing in the heat and strength of his long, lean length next to hers. 'Why didn't you invite your father to our wedding?'

'I thought it would be too awkward for my mother and our guests, particularly when Ciccio is fighting for a bigger divorce settlement because he stands to lose a lot of things that he's always taken for granted.'

'Concetta seems quite happy...well, for someone going through a divorce, that is,' Holly qualified ruefully.

'With my father gone she has a lot less stress in her life and for the first time she has her independence without the restriction of either a father or a husband. She loves her new home and the freedom she has there.'

'It's a new life for her,' Holly mused drowsily, thinking that her own new life was still in the honeymoon period and wouldn't really officially start until they returned to the *castello* the following day and embarked on a more normal routine.

'I didn't realise that marrying you would be a new beginning for me as well,' Vito admitted thoughtfully, acknowledging that he had not fully thought through the ramifications of marrying and becoming a parent. He had plunged into matrimony, dimly expecting life to go on as it always had only to learn that change was inevitable.

'Do you have regrets?' she whispered fearfully. 'Do you sometimes wish you were still single and unencumbered? I suppose you must.'

'I have no regrets when I'm in bed with you...not a single one.' Vito gazed down at her with dancing dark golden eyes alive with wolfish amusement. '*Sì*, I knew you'd be annoyed by that point but, *Dio mio*...at least I'm honest!'

And as his eyes laughed down at her, her heart swelled inside her and she knew, just *knew* in her very soul that she loved Vito. She loved him the way she had tried not to love him. She had tried so hard to protect herself from feeling more for Vito than he felt for her because that was the hard lesson she had learned in loving her unresponsive mother. You couldn't *make* a person care for you; you couldn't force those feelings.

In any case, it had crossed her mind more than once that Vito's emotions might be quite unavailable in the love category. Holly had met Vito on the rebound, shortly after his fiancée had ditched him. That Christmas theirs had been a classic rebound attraction. Was

Vito still in love with Marzia? Had he tried to return to the beautiful blonde during the fourteen months he and Holly had been apart? Had he mourned the loss of Marzia once he'd decided that he had to marry Holly for his son's sake? And how, when he never ever so much as mentioned the woman, could Holly possibly ask him to tell her honestly how he currently felt about Marzia?

She couldn't ask because she didn't think she could bear to live with the wrong answer.

CHAPTER TEN

TWO WEEKS LATER, Holly shuffled the messy pile of financial publications that Vito always left in his wake and lifted the other, more gossipy newspapers out to peruse. She flicked through the pages, thrilled when she was able to translate the occasional word of Italian.

Her knowledge of the language was slowly growing. She could manage simple interactions with their staff and greetings. Hopefully once she started proper Italian lessons with a local teacher later in the week her grasp of Italian would grow in leaps and bounds. After all, both her son and her husband would speak the language and she was determined not to be the odd one out. Vito's desire that their son should grow up bilingual was more likely to be successful if she learned Italian as well.

Abandoning the papers, she selected a magazine, flipping through glossy photographs of Italian celebrities she mostly didn't recognise until one picture in particular stopped her dead in her tracks. It was a photo of Marzia wearing the most fabulous sparkling ballgown with Vito by her side. She frowned and stared down at it with such intensity that she literally saw spots appear in front of her eyes. She struggled to translate the blurb

beneath the picture. It appeared to be recent and it had
been taken at some party. The previous week, Vito had
spent two nights at his Florence apartment because he
had said he was working late. Well, the first time he
had been working late, the second time he had actually
said that he had to attend a very boring dinner, which
invariably would drag on into the early hours...

For dinner, read dinner *dance*, she reflected unhappily. Her entire attention was welded to the photo. Vito
and Marzia had been captured at what appeared to be a
formal dance with their arms in the air as if their hands
had just parted from a clasp. Both of them were smiling. And my goodness, didn't Marzia look ravishing?
Not a blonde hair out of place. Holly's fingers crept up
to finger through her own tumbled mane. She studied
Marzia's perfectly made-up face and thought about her
own careless beauty routine, which often consisted of
little more than eyeliner, blush and lip gloss. Looking
at that gorgeous dress, she glanced down at her own
casual silky tee and skirt and low-heeled sandals. She
was dressed very nicely indeed in expensive garments
but there wasn't even a hint of glamour or sequinned
sparkle in her appearance.

Maybe it had only been one dance that Marzia and
Vito had shared. And of course they had been photo-
graphed for such a potentially awkward moment between former partners was always of interest to others.
And they were smiling and happy together. Why not?
Her heart had shrunk into a tight, threatened lump inside her chest and her tummy felt as though it were
filled with concrete. Vito had spent a couple of years
with Marzia. They knew each other well and why
should they be enemies? There was no reason why they

shouldn't dance together and treat each other like old friends, was there?

Vito hadn't broken any rules. He hadn't told her any lies. All right, he hadn't mentioned the dancing or seeing Marzia, but then he never mentioned his ex, a reality that had made it very difficult for Holly to tackle the subject. Wasn't Vito entitled to his privacy in relation to past relationships? In any case he was not the kind of man who would comfortably open up about previous lovers. Her eyes stung with tears because trying to be reasonable and take a sensible overview was such a challenge for her at that moment.

At the heart of her reaction, Holly registered, was Marzia's sheer glamour and her own sense of inadequacy. Holly didn't do glamour, had never even tried. The closest she had ever got to glamour was a Santa outfit. But what if that kind of gloss, *Marzia's* gloss, was what Vito really liked and admired?

Obviously she had to confront him about the photo and there would probably be a perfectly reasonable explanation about why he had said nothing…

'I knew you would make a fuss,' Vito would be able to point out quite rightly.

She was a jealous cow and he probably sensed that. Although she had never been competitive with other women, having a rival that beautiful and sophisticated could only be hurtful and intimidating. She loved Vito so much and was painfully aware that he did not love her. In addition, she was always guiltily conscious that she had won her wedding ring purely by default. Vito had married her because she was the mother of his son.

Mother of his son, Holly repeated inwardly. Not a very sexy label, certainly not very glamorous. But it didn't have to be that way, she reasoned ruefully. She could walk that extra mile, she could make the effort and dress up too. But she needed the excuse of an occasion, didn't she? Well, at least to begin with... On her passage across the hall, she spoke to Silvestro and told him that she would like a special romantic meal to be served for dinner.

Silvestro positively glowed with approval and she went upstairs to go through her new wardrobe and select the fanciest dress she owned. In the oddest way she would have liked to put on a Santa outfit for Vito again but it wouldn't work out of season. She would tackle Vito the moment he came home. She wouldn't give him time to regroup and come up with evasions or excuses. What she wanted most of all was honesty. He needed to tell her how he truly felt about Marzia and they would proceed from that point.

Did he still have feelings for the beautiful blonde? How would she cope if he admitted that? Well, she would have to cope. Her life, Vito's and Angelo's were inextricably bound to the stability of their marriage. Would he want a separation? A divorce? Her brain was making giant leaps into disaster zones and she told herself off for the catastrophic effect that photo had had on her imagination and her confidence. Since when had she chosen to lie down and die rather than fight?

From the dressing room she extracted the hand-embroidered full-length dress, which glittered with sparkling beads below the lights. It definitely belonged in the glamour category.

Vito knew something strange was afoot the instant he walked into the hall of the *castello* and Silvestro gave him a huge smile. Silvestro had the face of a sad sheep-dog and was not prone to smiling.

'The *signora* is on the way downstairs...' he was informed.

Vito blinked and then he saw Holly as he had only seen her on their wedding day, and quite naturally he stared. She drifted down the staircase in a fantastic dress that seemed to float airily round her hourglass curves. It was the sort of gown a woman wore to a ball and Vito suffered a stark instant of very male panic. Why was she all dressed up? What had he forgotten? Were they supposed to be going out somewhere? What special date had slipped past him unnoticed?

Silvestro spread wide the dining-room door and Vito saw the table set in a pool of candlelight and flowers and thought...what the hell? He spun back as Holly drew level with him, her blue eyes bright but her small face oddly tight and expressionless. A pang ran through Vito's long, lean frame because he was accustomed to his wife greeting him at the end of the day as though he had been absent for a week...and in truth he thoroughly enjoyed the wholehearted affection she showered on both him and his son.

'You look magnificent, *bellezza mia*,' Vito declared, while frantically wondering what occasion he had overlooked and how he could possibly cover up that reality rather than hurt Holly's feelings by admitting his ignorance.

She was so vulnerable sometimes. He saw that sensitivity in her and marvelled that she retained it even after all the disappointments life had faced her with. His primary role was to protect Holly from hurt and disillusionment. He didn't want her to lose her innocence. He didn't want her to turn cynical or bitter. But most of all he never ever wanted to be the man who disillusioned her.

'Glad you like the dress,' Holly said a tad woodenly. 'Shall we sit down?'

'I'm no match for your elegance without a shower and a change of clothes,' Vito pointed out with a slight line dividing his black brows into the beginnings of a frown because her odd behaviour was frustrating him.

'Please sit down. We'll have a drink,' Holly suggested, because she had laid that photo of Marzia and him at his place at the table and she was keen for him to see it before she lost her nerve at confronting him in what was starting to feel a little like a badly planned head-on collision.

Maybe she should have been less confrontational and given him warning. Only not if the price of that was Vito coming up with a polite story that went nowhere near the actual truth. She didn't believe he would lie to her but he wouldn't want to upset her and he would pick and choose words to persuade her in a devious way that her concerns were nonsensical.

Vito was on the edge of arguing until he glimpsed the photo, and its appearance was so unexpected that it stupefied him. He stared down at the photo of himself dancing with Marzia in wonderment while Silvestro poured his wine. Why were they apparently celebrating this inappropriate photograph with rose petals scattered across the table and the finest wine? His frown of incomprehension deepened.

'What is this?' he demanded with an abruptness that startled Holly as he swept up the photo.

Consternation gripped Holly because he didn't sound

puzzled, he sounded downright angry. 'I wanted to ask you to explain that picture,' she muttered warily.

'So you set me up with some sort of a romantic dinner and tell me I can't have a shower? And sit me down with a photo of my ex?' Vito exclaimed incredulously. 'This is more than a little weird, Holly!'

Legs turning wobbly as she encountered scorching dark golden eyes of enquiry, Holly dropped reluctantly down into her chair. 'I'm sorry. I just wanted to get it over with and I wanted you to say exactly what's on your mind.'

'Weird!' Vito repeated with an emphatic lack of inhibition, crumpling the photo into a ball of crushed paper and firing it into the fire burning merrily across the room. 'Where did you get that photograph from and when did you see it?'

Holly sketched out the details, her heart beating very fast. She hadn't expected to feel guilty but now she did because taking Vito by surprise had only annoyed him.

'Today?' Vito stressed in astonishment. 'But that photo is at least three years old!'

'Three years old…' Holly's voice trailed off as she studied him in disbelief.

'It was taken at our engagement party. Why on earth would it be printed again now?' he questioned.

Holly scrambled out of her seat and pelted off to find the magazine she had cut the photo from. Reappearing, she planted it into Vito's outstretched hand while Silvestro struggled to set out the first course of the meal.

'Per l'amor di Dio…' Vito groaned. 'You need to learn to read Italian!'

'It's not going to happen overnight,' she grumbled.

'That photo was quite cleverly utilised to symbolise

the fact that I have now cut my ties to the Ravello Investment Bank,' Vito framed in flat explanation. 'Note the way our hands are pictured apart...'

'What does the Ravello Bank have to do with anything? What ties?'

'Marzia is a Ravello,' Vito informed her drily. 'When we got engaged I agreed to act as an investment adviser to the Ravello Bank. When Marzia ditched me her father begged me to retain the position as Ravello was going through a crisis and my resignation would have created talk and blighted their prospects even more.'

Holly blinked. She had become very pale. 'I had no idea you had any business links to Marzia and her family.'

'As of yesterday I *don't*. I resigned the position and they have hired the man I recommended to take my place. Once you and I were married it no longer felt appropriate for Marzia's family and mine to retain that business link,' Vito pointed out wryly.

Holly had been blindsided by an element of Vito's former relationship with Marzia that she could not have known about. A business connection, *not* a personal one. 'You know, I assumed that that was a recent picture of you with Marzia,' Holly confided. 'I thought that dinner you mentioned last week must have been a dinner dance.'

'Had it been I would have taken you with me or bowed out early to get home to you. As it was I was landed with a group of visiting government representatives, whose company I found as exciting as watching paint dry,' Vito told her drily and pushed back his chair. 'May I have my shower now?'

'No, we can't just abandon dinner!' Holly breathed

in dismay. 'Not when Francisco has gone to so much trouble to make us a memorable meal.'

'So, you've been down to the kitchen and have finally met our chef?' Vito gathered in some amusement.

'Yes, he's a real charmer, isn't he?'

'I'm sure he can reheat the food,' Vito pronounced impatiently.

'But we haven't finished talking yet,' Holly protested, all her expectations thrown by Vito's eminently down-to-earth explanation of that photo and its meaning.

'Why are you dressed as though you're about to attend a costume ball?' Vito shot at her.

Holly went red. 'I wanted to show you that if I made the effort I could polish up and look all glam like Marzia.'

Vito groaned out loud. 'You look amazing but I don't want you to look all glam like Marzia.'

'But you bought me all those fancy clothes…'

'Only to cover every possible occasion. And when would you have bothered going shopping?' Vito enquired drily. 'You hate shopping for clothes.'

Holly compressed her lips. 'You don't like me glammed up? Or you don't want me copying Marzia?'

'Both,' Vito told her levelly as he signalled Silvestro and rose from his chair again. 'I like you just to be yourself. You're never fake. I *hate* fake. But why did you think I would be out dancing any place with Marzia?'

'What are you doing?' Holly gasped as he scooped her bodily out of her seat.

'I'm going for my after-work shower and you're either coming in with me, which would sacrifice all the effort you have gone to, or you're waiting in bed for me,' Vito informed her cheerfully.

'I thought you still cared for Marzia,' Holly finally confessed on the way up the stairs. 'I thought you might still love her.'

Vito grunted with effort as he reached the landing. 'I can carry you upstairs but I can't talk while I'm doing it,' he confided. 'I never loved Marzia.'

'But you got engaged to her... You *lived* with her!'

'Yes, and what an eye-opening experience that was!' Vito admitted, thrusting wide the door of their bedroom. 'I asked her to marry me in the first place because she was everything my grandfather told me I should look for in a wife. I wasn't in love with her and when we lived together I discovered that we had nothing in common. I don't want to dance the night away as if I'm still in my twenties but Marzia does. She has to have other people around all the time. She likes to shop every day and will avoid any activity that wrecks her hair... up to and including a walk on a windy day and sex.'

'Oh...' Open-mouthed and taken aback by that information, Holly fell very still as Vito ran down the zip on her dress.

'I was relieved when she ditched me. Not very gallant but it's the truth. We weren't suited.'

'Was my ring...? I've always wanted to ask,' Holly interrupted, extending her ring finger. 'Was it Marzia's before you gave it to me?'

An ebony brow shot up. 'Are you joking? Marzia didn't return her engagement ring and even if she had I hope I would've had more class than to ask you to wear it.'

'You *never* loved her?' Holly was challenged to credit that fact because it ran contrary to everything she had assumed about his engagement.

'When I met Marzia, I had never been in love in my life,' Vito admitted ruefully. 'I got burned young watching my mother trying to persuade my father to love her. I spent my twenties waiting to fall in love, convinced someone special would eventually appear. But it didn't happen and I was convinced it never would. I decided I was probably too practical to fall in love. That's why I got engaged to Marzia the week after my thirtieth birthday. At the time she looked like the best bet I had. Similar banking family and background.'

'My word…that sounds almost…almost callous,' Holly murmured in shock. 'Like choosing the best offer at the supermarket.'

'If it's any consolation I'm pretty sure Marzia settled for me because I'm extremely wealthy.'

Vito yanked loose his tie and shed his jacket. Holly's dress slid down her shoulders and for an instant she stopped its downward progress and then she let it go and shimmied out of it. In many ways she was still in shock from Vito's honesty. He had never fallen in love? Not even with the gorgeous Marzia, who by all accounts had irritated him in spite of her pedigreed background and family. She swallowed hard, trying not to wonder how much she irritated him.

'You're definitely not joining me in the shower,' Vito breathed in a roughened undertone as he took in the coffee-coloured silk lingerie she sported below the dress that had tumbled round her feet. 'You can't deprive me of the fun of taking those off.'

His shirt fell on the floor and she lifted it and the trousers that were abandoned just as untidily to drape them on a chair along with her dress. Sharing a bedroom with a male as organised as Vito had made her clean up her bad habits. Vito had paused to rifle through his jacket and he strode back to her to stuff a jewellery case unceremoniously into her hand. 'I saw it online, thought you'd like it.'

'Oh…' Holly flipped open the case on a diamond-studded bracelet with a delicate little Christmas tree charm attached. 'Oh, that's very pretty.'

'It's very *you*, isn't it?' Vito remarked smugly.

'Why didn't you give it to me downstairs over dinner?' Holly exclaimed, struggling to attach it to her wrist until he stepped forward to clasp it for her.

'I forgot about it. You swanning down to greet me dressed like Marie Antoinette put it right out of my mind.'

'And then you just virtually threw it at me,' Holly lamented. 'There's a more personal way of giving a gift.'

'You mean romantic.' Vito sighed as he strode into the en-suite bathroom, still characteristically set on having his shower. 'Shouldn't the thought *behind* the gift count more?'

Holly thought about that and then walked to the bathroom doorway to sigh. 'You're right. I'm sorry. It's a cute, thoughtful present and I love it. Thank you.'

'My thank you was your face. It lit up like a child's when you saw the Christmas tree,' Vito confided with amusement before he turned the water on.

Holly kicked off her shoes, stared down appreciatively at the bracelet encircling her wrist and lay down on the bed. He had never loved Marzia. Marzia was wiped from Holly's standard stock of worries for ever. Marzia was the past—a past Vito neither missed nor wanted to revisit. That, she decided, was a very encouraging discovery.

All of a sudden hiding her love, being so painfully careful not to let those words escape in moments of joy, seemed almost mean and dishonest. Vito loved Angelo so freely. She witnessed that every day. Her husband hadn't even had to try to love his son and Angelo loved his father back. Perhaps in time Vito could come to love her too, she reflected hopefully. When he had told her that he much preferred her to just be herself around him without the fancy clothes or any airs her heart had taken wings. He liked her as she was. Wasn't that wonderful?

Vito strode out of the en suite, still towelling dry his hair. 'We'll have a very special Christmas this year. For the first time I'll happily celebrate the season. That's the effect you and Angelo have had on my Scrooge-like outlook.'

'I'm grateful because I will always love Christmas.'

'Because that's how we met,' Vito reasoned. 'And I've never forgotten how appealing you looked dressing that little tree at the cottage.'

'Is that so? And yet you made me fight for the opportunity,' Holly reminded him.

'You gave me a fresh look at the world and it's never been the same since,' Vito intoned very seriously as he settled down on the bed beside her and closed her into his arms.

'Meaning?'

'Remember I said I went through my twenties waiting for someone special to appear?'

Holly nodded and rubbed her cheek against a damp bronzed shoulder.

'And then she came along when I was thirty-one years old and, unfortunately, incredibly wary and set in my ways.'

Her brow furrowed because she thought she had missed a line somewhere. '*Who* came along?'

'You did,' Vito pointed out gently. 'And I wasn't waiting or looking for love any more, and my practical engagement had gone belly-up. So, when you appeared and you made me feel strange I didn't recognise that it was special. The sex was incredible but I was blind to the fact that everything else was incredible too.'

'I made you feel...*strange*?' Holly exclaimed in dismay.

'Confused, unsure of myself. I behaved differently with you, I *felt* more with you...and it troubled me. So, like an idiot, I walked away from what I didn't understand,' he completed.

'I wish you'd found my note,' Holly lamented.

'When you walked out first, I told myself that was for the best, that we could never work in the real world. But we *do* work,' Vito told her with quiet satisfaction. 'We work like a dream on every level and I have never been as happy as I am now...'

Holly was thinking about what he had said and a spark of excitement lit inside her.

'If you and Angelo hadn't found me again, where would I be now? The heart and soul of my world was the Zaffari Bank but the bank wasn't enough to satisfy me.'

'Are you trying to tell me that you fell for me that night?' Holly whispered shakily.

'Well, if you have to ask, obviously I'm not doing a very good job of the telling.' Vito groaned. 'What you made me feel unnerved me. I wouldn't even let myself try to trace you because I was too proud. If you didn't want me I wasn't going to chase after you. I tried very hard to forget that night. I even tried to sleep with other women.'

'And how did that go?' Holly broke in to demand.

'It didn't. I made excuses to myself that I was stressed, overtired. I had endless fantasies about you.'

'Me…the temptress,' Holly framed blissfully. 'Who would ever have thought it?'

'You're the love of my life…the *only* love I have ever had,' Vito husked, clamping her to his long, powerful length with strong arms. 'And I fell hard. I fell *so* hard I can't imagine ever living without you and our son. You have brought passion and fun into my daily life and I never had either before.'

'I love you too,' Holly muttered almost shyly.

Vito smiled down at her with burnished golden eyes and her heart skipped a beat. He kissed her with hot, hungry fervour and she ran out of breath. He lifted his tousled dark head and murmured, 'I have one special request. Would you consider having another child?'

'Another?' Holly gasped in astonishment.

'Not immediately,' Vito hastened to assure her. 'I want to share your next pregnancy, *be* there when my child is born, and experience everything I missed out on with our son. If you employ an assistant, even if you get pregnant I don't see why you shouldn't still be able to concentrate on your interior design plan.'

Holly smiled at that prospect. Her very successful bedroom project had quickly spread to include other major rooms at the *castello*. She had had the adjoining reception room done in toning colours before moving on to attack the scarlet Victorian dining room. At present she was well aware that the *castello* was large enough to offer her the chance to utilise her talents and gain proper experience before she considered moving on to tackle outside projects.

'I'll think about another baby,' she told him thoughtfully. 'I would prefer Angelo not to be an only child.'

Vito stared down at her as she gazed up at him with starry eyes. *He loves me, he loves me, he* loves *me,* she was thinking on a happy high. She ran an appreciative hand up over a long, muscular, hair-roughened thigh and sensible conversation ceased around that point. Vito told her he loved her. Holly told him she loved him too. No sooner had they exchanged those sentiments than they both succumbed to an overwhelming desire to dispel the tension with the passion they shared.

Long after, Vito lay studying Holly as she slept, marvelling at how happy he felt. He wondered if he could persuade her into another sexy Santa outfit at Christmas and wondered if it would be a little pushy to buy one for her. Pushiness came so naturally to him that he soon convinced himself that his laid-back bride would simply laugh.

He curved an arm round her slight body.

'Love you…' Holly mumbled automatically.

Vito smiled. 'Love you. You're my happy-ever-after, *amata mia.*'

EPILOGUE

VITO STRODE THROUGH the door and was immediately engulfed in the flying energy of his son, who flung himself at his knees in a classic tackle. Angelo started chattering in a hail of words, only a handful of which were in distinguishable Italian and occasional ones were in English. *Mamma* figured a lot. *Nonna*, as he called his grandmother Concetta, figured too. If Angelo was to be believed, he, his mother and his grandmother had spent the afternoon feeding a dinosaur. A very small dinosaur was waved in Vito's general direction and comprehension set in as he crouched down to dutifully admire the toy.

A giant Christmas tree adorned the hall. It was festooned with ornaments and lights. There were no gifts heaped below the branches because Angelo loved to rip off wrapping paper. Silvestro had been heard to tell a tenant that the Zaffaris were having 'an English Christmas', and Vito's chef, Francisco, had been feeding them turkey for weeks as he fine-tuned his recipes to provide them with an English banquet on Christmas Day. In respect of the Italian traditions, Angelo would receive *la calza*—a stocking full of sweets. The red-suited Babbo Natale would obviously visit on Christmas Eve, but the kind-hearted Italian witch La Befana, who searched for the Christ child in all the houses, would visit at Epiphany with more gifts.

Vito breathed in deep as he saw a small figure clad in white-fur-trimmed scarlet appear at the top of the stairs. 'You're not wearing your hat,' he complained.

Holly stopped midway and jammed it on over her mane of hair and made a face at him. 'Satisfied now?'

Vito angled a lazy, sexy smile at her. 'Don't I have to wait until bedtime for that?'

'Maybe I'll suggest an early night.' Holly remained anchored two steps up so that she was almost level with him.

Vito took the invitation, leaning down to claim that lush pink mouth that he still fantasised about and curving his hands to the swell of her hips to lift her up into his arms. Her hands locked round his neck with satisfying possessiveness and held him fast. He could feel the slight bump of the baby she was carrying against his stomach and he smiled as he lifted his head again.

'I love you,' he groaned.

'Love you madly.' Holly felt ridiculously intoxicated and happy. One kiss from Vito could do that, two were irresistible, and three would only end with her dragging him up the stairs. Evidently falling pregnant sooner than they had expected had done nothing to cool her husband's desire for her and that truly did make her feel as alluring as some legendary temptress. That was very welcome to a woman who was five months pregnant and subject to all the usual aches and complaints of her condition.

Her redecoration schemes at the *castello* had led to an approach from an exclusive interiors magazine, which had taken a whole host of photos. The glossy photo spread and the accompanying article had ensured that within days of the magazine going on sale, Holly was inundated with exciting offers of design work.

This, however, was their first family Christmas and she was revelling in every detail because Vito had really thrown himself into the spirit of the holidays and she didn't think it was solely because he had become a father. She reckoned he had put his sour childhood memories of Christmas behind him. His mother, recently divorced, was joining their festivities and hugely excited about the second grandchild on the way.

'Please tell me turkey isn't on the menu again tonight,' Vito murmured.

'No, we're having steak. I told Francisco I fancied steak,' she admitted.

'When are our guests arriving?' Vito prompted.

'Well, they were supposed to be here for dinner but Apollo's social secretary rang to say they would be late. Why does he need a social secretary?'

'He's always got hundreds of invitations and he's never at home.' Vito paused. 'I appreciate you being willing to give him another chance.'

Holly gave him a soothing smile that concealed her tension. It was past time to forgive and forget—she knew that. After all, Apollo was Vito's closest friend, but Holly had only seen him twice since their wedding. And when she had made the mistake of voicing her opinion on what he considered to be his private business it had been awkward as hell. But she was madly curious to see who he was bringing with him as a guest. Another leggy underwear model? Or his *wife*?

That, Holly supposed, would be another story...

* * * * *

MILLS & BOON®
Hardback – November 2016

ROMANCE

Di Sione's Virgin Mistress	Sharon Kendrick
Snowbound with His Innocent Temptation	Cathy Williams
The Italian's Christmas Child	Lynne Graham
A Diamond for Del Rio's Housekeeper	Susan Stephens
Claiming His Christmas Consequence	Michelle Smart
One Night with Gael	Maya Blake
Married for the Italian's Heir	Rachael Thomas
Unwrapping His Convenient Fiancée	Melanie Milburne
Christmas Baby for the Princess	Barbara Wallace
Greek Tycoon's Mistletoe Proposal	Kandy Shepherd
The Billionaire's Prize	Rebecca Winters
The Earl's Snow-Kissed Proposal	Nina Milne
The Nurse's Christmas Gift	Tina Beckett
The Midwife's Pregnancy Miracle	Kate Hardy
Their First Family Christmas	Alison Roberts
The Nightshift Before Christmas	Annie O'Neil
It Started at Christmas...	Janice Lynn
Unwrapped by the Duke	Amy Ruttan
Hold Me, Cowboy	Maisey Yates
Holiday Baby Scandal	Jules Bennett

MILLS & BOON®
Large Print – November 2016

ROMANCE

Di Sione's Innocent Conquest	Carol Marinelli
A Virgin for Vasquez	Cathy Williams
The Billionaire's Ruthless Affair	Miranda Lee
Master of Her Innocence	Chantelle Shaw
Moretti's Marriage Command	Kate Hewitt
The Flaw in Raffaele's Revenge	Annie West
Bought by Her Italian Boss	Dani Collins
Wedded for His Royal Duty	Susan Meier
His Cinderella Heiress	Marion Lennox
The Bridesmaid's Baby Bump	Kandy Shepherd
Bound by the Unborn Baby	Bella Bucannon

HISTORICAL

The Unexpected Marriage of Gabriel Stone	Louise Allen
The Outcast's Redemption	Sarah Mallory
Claiming the Chaperon's Heart	Anne Herries
Commanded by the French Duke	Meriel Fuller
Unbuttoning the Innocent Miss	Bronwyn Scott

MEDICAL

Tempted by Hollywood's Top Doc	Louisa George
Perfect Rivals...	Amy Ruttan
English Rose in the Outback	Lucy Clark
A Family for Chloe	Lucy Clark
The Doctor's Baby Secret	Scarlet Wilson
Married for the Boss's Baby	Susan Carlisle

MILLS & BOON®
Hardback – December 2016

ROMANCE

A Di Sione for the Greek's Pleasure	Kate Hewitt
The Prince's Pregnant Mistress	Maisey Yates
The Greek's Christmas Bride	Lynne Graham
The Guardian's Virgin Ward	Caitlin Crews
A Royal Vow of Convenience	Sharon Kendrick
The Desert King's Secret Heir	Annie West
Married for the Sheikh's Duty	Tara Pammi
Surrendering to the Vengeful Italian	Angela Bissell
Winter Wedding for the Prince	Barbara Wallace
Christmas in the Boss's Castle	Scarlet Wilson
Her Festive Doorstep Baby	Kate Hardy
Holiday with the Mystery Italian	Ellie Darkins
White Christmas for the Single Mum	Susanne Hampton
A Royal Baby for Christmas	Scarlet Wilson
Playboy on Her Christmas List	Carol Marinelli
The Army Doc's Baby Bombshell	Sue MacKay
The Doctor's Sleigh Bell Proposal	Susan Carlisle
The Baby Proposal	Andrea Laurence
Maid Under the Mistletoe	Maureen Child

MILLS & BOON®
Large Print – December 2016

ROMANCE

The Di Sione Secret Baby	Maya Blake
Carides's Forgotten Wife	Maisey Yates
The Playboy's Ruthless Pursuit	Miranda Lee
His Mistress for a Week	Melanie Milburne
Crowned for the Prince's Heir	Sharon Kendrick
In the Sheikh's Service	Susan Stephens
Marrying Her Royal Enemy	Jennifer Hayward
An Unlikely Bride for the Billionaire	Michelle Douglas
Falling for the Secret Millionaire	Kate Hardy
The Forbidden Prince	Alison Roberts
The Best Man's Guarded Heart	Katrina Cudmore

HISTORICAL

Sheikh's Mail-Order Bride	Marguerite Kaye
Miss Marianne's Disgrace	Georgie Lee
Her Enemy at the Altar	Virginia Heath
Enslaved by the Desert Trader	Greta Gilbert
Royalist on the Run	Helen Dickson

MEDICAL

The Prince and the Midwife	Robin Gianna
His Pregnant Sleeping Beauty	Lynne Marshall
One Night, Twin Consequences	Annie O'Neil
Twin Surprise for the Single Doc	Susanne Hampton
The Doctor's Forbidden Fling	Karin Baine
The Army Doc's Secret Wife	Charlotte Hawkes

MILLS & BOON®

Why shop at millsandboon.co.uk?

Each year, thousands of romance readers find their perfect read at millsandboon.co.uk. That's because we're passionate about bringing you the very best romantic fiction. Here are some of the advantages of shopping at www.millsandboon.co.uk:

* **Get new books first**—you'll be able to buy your favourite books one month before they hit the shops

* **Get exclusive discounts**—you'll also be able to buy our specially created monthly collections, with up to 50% off the RRP

* **Find your favourite authors**—latest news, interviews and new releases for all your favourite authors and series on our website, plus ideas for what to try next

* **Join in**—once you've bought your favourite books, don't forget to register with us to rate, review and join in the discussions

Visit **www.millsandboon.co.uk**
for all this and more today!